The Woman Under the Ground

And Other Stories

Megan Taylor

Weathervane Press

Weathervane Press

Published in 2014 by Weathervane Press

www.weathervanepress.co.uk

ISBN 978 0 9562193 9 8

Cover design and all illustrations © Nikki Pinder
www.nikkipinder.co.uk

Printed by Lightning Source

For Giselle, with love

The following short stories, or versions of these stories, have previously featured in the competitions, publications and readings listed below:

School Run – longlisted in The Asham Award

Berrycake – longlisted in the Cinnamon Press Short Story Competition 2013 & shortlisted in the Writers' Forum Competition 2014

The Dining Room Ghost – selected for reading at Mayhem Halloween Film Festival 2012 at Nottingham's Broadway Cinema

Coach Trip – Highly Commended in the Manchester Fiction Prize 2013

The Woman Under the Ground – longlisted in the Cinnamon Press Short Story Competition 2011 and published in the short story anthology 'Weird Love', edited by David Chadwick & Nicky Harlow, Pandril Press, 2013

The Insect Room – published in Manchester Metropolitan University's 'Muse 7', 2010

On the Island – longlisted in BBC Radio 4's Opening Lines Competition, 2014

Rash – shortlisted in the Willesden Herald Competition 2014 and published in 'Willesden Herald: New Short Stories 8', edited by Steve Moran, Pretend Genius Press, 2014

Bones – selected for reading at Mayhem Halloween Film Festival 2013 at Nottingham's Broadway Cinema and shortlisted in the Synaesthesia Short Story Competition 2014

Contents

School Run

There are voices in my head.

"Watch out," they say as I round the corner, as the wind rushes towards me, tasting of diesel and dead leaves.

"There they are," the voices tell me.

"Who?" I ask, but of course I know exactly who they mean.

There's a gang of them, standing at the school gates. Some have blond hair with black roots; others are streaked with red or striped grey. They wear leggings and jeans, and boots, or they wear trainers. A tall leather coat leans against a dumpy fake fur. They're talking. Their sounds huff towards me with their fleecy cigarette-smoke breath.

As I approach, they turn around, in turn. Peachy lipstick mouths on jolting clockwork heads – I try to change my own face. I'm searching for a smile.

"Don't listen to them," the voices say. "Keep going..."

I feel myself growing bigger and then bigger. Their eyes blink at me too fast, so that all I can see, for a moment, is a whir of lashes – thick lashes around gleaming eyes, like the eyes in silent movies. Soon I'll be on top of them.

"Don't let them touch you!"

"*Shhhh*," I say, but it's hopeless. I'm helpless. The voices never listen back.

I've nearly reached the gate. The women lean closer, a watching knot. From a distance, it might look as though I'm standing among them quite deliberately.

I mustn't stare, but I can't help it. I'm right in the middle of their mass, at their very heart.

"*Keep walking.*"

I see their shiny hands, a pair of tight-tight gloves and a flash of vinyl nails. My own fists are clenched deep inside my pockets. Their stringent perfume makes me wince. They shake back their hair and stamp like horses. Steam pours out of them, between their noses and their flapping mouths.

"Excuse me," I say, inching past a padded elbow and two staring nylon breasts. "Excuse me please, I must get by."

"What's that, Love?" says one.

The words puff out and then explode in the sharp winter air. I picture them, transformed from something soft into a sudden glittering, like broken glass. I can't answer. Instead I focus on the playground, rolling out beyond them. And beyond.

"Don't talk to them," the voices tell me.

"Be quiet," I hiss. "Shut up."

A baby gazes up at me from a pram. It has the knowing, watery eyes of a gorilla-baby in a zoo, a tragic and resigned expression, framed by a woolly green blanket. There's a dummy in its mouth, pinning it still.

"Don't look," the voices say and I don't, but the baby's eyes skip after me. Two cold pebbles catching my neck.

But it's all right; the women are falling back now like heavy curtains, their bags and sleeves and coattails swinging wearily apart. And I've made it. I'm through, at last.

I take in the playground slowly, as I always do, in little cautious glances. I see the monkey bars and the benches, dark and glistening from the rain at lunch. I see the rusted drinking taps and the netball hoop. The grey ground with its painted grids and numbers, half-worn away. I smell the wet, rising up from the bricks and wood and concrete, a dense, bloodlike odour that I can also taste; it rings in the chinks between my teeth. I move on quickly before the voices grab their chance. Directly ahead, there's a single, leafless, fenced-in tree.

I blink up to where the criss-cross of bare branches stretches, fishnet tights torn across the sky. A sky that's already sorry-looking, stretch-marked and bruised. There's a skipping rope hanging from the highest branches. As I watch, it starts to spin. The wind whispers, circling us both.

And there's the school, of course: the school, with its brown bricks and silver windows. A row of carefully closed doors.

My daughter's behind one of them. *That one*, with the peeling paint. Thankfully, her classroom is on ground level, not like mine used to be, set way up on the second floor. Still, she's far enough away, my daughter; she's sealed up tight.

It's the end of the day, so it'll be all crossed legs and hands-in-laps and no one really listening to the story. That time when you can't wait to leave; you're desperate to leave, to break outside, to run... And the girl behind you is leaning closer, a pointed compass or twisted paperclip, something small and sharp and shiny, hidden in her fist.

But whatever happens, you'll try not to move. You will set your face and go on staring at the teacher. You can't afford to let anything slip –

Though "*loon*," the girl might say, unless it's the boy who is sitting next to her. Either way, her voice

13

will emerge hot and sugary, smelling thickly of the rounded yellow biscuits they gave everyone at lunch.

"Loony-Tunes," she'll mutter: "Nutter..."

With a series of dull thuds, the heavy doors fall open and out the children run. A single solid rush of hair and hoods and bags and feet. Laughter and outrage whirl up into the mottled sky. A tornado of sound, high-pitched and clamouring, only frayed and stuttering about its edges.

My daughter appears. She hovers, with her little arms wrapped around her little waist. She stands as though she is holding herself together, as though she's broken –

But her hair glows. It is pale blond and gorgeous, like the dense creamy fur on a cat's belly. For a moment, I have to fight the urge to bury my face in it, to hide there.

But, "M-mum," she's saying. "*Mum*. Mrs Sawyer wants to see you."

Mrs Sawyer is the teacher. She is waiting in the doorway, the classroom a warm yellow square against her back.

"Ms Waters? Ms Waters?" she calls.

Her voice is sweet and sticky, like the paper we used to hang up in the summer, to catch flies. Her eyes are wide and blue and careful. I can tell that she knows all about me, about who I am. Obviously, people will have told her. *Chat, chat, chat...* They just can't help it.

My own voices remain quiet, but I can feel them in me all the same. Hunched together, waiting.

"Go on, Mum," Anna says.

She's sounding calm. And clear. "A big *slow* voice", the speech therapist told her. She holds her hands together now, fingers wrapped in fingers.

"Mum," she says. "Mum, p-please."

I go over to the teacher with her blue, waiting eyes and she nods and smiles a creeping smile. She starts talking almost immediately. *Blah, blah, blah.* Obviously I don't hear her, but I smile and nod right back and I think how we're like twin, bobbing puppets, opposite ends of some ticking pendulum. We nod and smile, nod and smile.

It'll be something about a P.E. kit or no dinner money or a trip somewhere, in a coach. It doesn't matter. Anna will explain her to me later.

I watch Anna pulling up her hood, blocking off her ears.

When she was smaller and used to fall asleep inside my lap, I'd count Anna's freckles to keep us safe. There were seventy-one freckles on her face and neck. I used to think that if I joined them up with a felt-tip pen, I might reveal a secret picture, or some coded message. She's full of secrets, my Anna, but she's reliable too. Her name is the same whichever way you look at it.

I can't see her freckles now. She's looking at my shoes.

And: "Anna!" someone calls. "An-*na.*"

I still like the way it sounds.

But there are two of them. They have glossy brown hair with fuzzy clips and sparkles. Smoke curls out of their mouths as they bounce across the grey, but it's only from the cold.

"Anna," they say, "come here a minute. Come with us."

My hand goes out and clamps down hard on my daughter's shoulder. She's quiet beneath it, warm and still. The teacher carries on talking, but I'm not looking at her. I'm looking at these girls. They have broad clean smiles that could swallow you up – shiny-sharp teeth, whiter than white. Snapping-bright.

"It's ok," Anna says, in her big, slow voice. "They're my friends."

What can I do? I let her go. And the teacher keeps on chatting, on and on. She rubs one long hand across her throat as she speaks. She leaves a crimson stripe behind, but I don't look at her for long. My gaze is on Anna as the three of them stride away, to some precious private corner of their playground.

Seventy-one freckles, I think. *Please be safe.*

"But you know what little girls are," the voices say, all too happy to be back.

I shake my head as if I can knock them down, as if I'm the one in charge. I gaze past the teacher's bony shoulder, into the yellow square of her world. It's just as I have pictured it. For weeks, I think. For years.

"You *know*," they say.

The plastic chairs with their cold metal legs are stacked haphazardly on the tables. There are picture books contained in a wire rack, their pages bent and tattered where they've been rammed back in too quickly. And there's already an old woman in the corner unloading a mop and bucket from her trolley. She wears a thin blue overall and tangerine lipstick. Nothing much has changed.

Even the radiators are the same. They're still huge, still coated in that thick, chipped paint. It comes back to me how they were always either scalding-hot or freezing – and how the pipes would murmur

16

continually, a stream of nonsense-messages like Chinese Whispers. For a while, I had thought that the voices might have been a part of them, right up until –

"*Go*," they told me, that last afternoon. "Go on," they said. "*Run.*"

That afternoon when I couldn't do it anymore, the sitting-still thing, the listening. Not with those kids, cross-legged behind me –

"*Hey, Loony-Tunes. Nutter –*"

Their sharp words and then a sharper pressure, their secret metal digging at my back.

And so I had stood up in the middle of Carpet Time. And they'd all looked at me, the teacher too. Everywhere, dark eyes and open lips.

"Go" the voices said. "Go, now!"

And so I did.

I *did*, although everyone was staring at me and then grabbing for me. *Shouting.* There was some laughter too – I remember that, and the teacher squawking, bobbing on her feet. So much noise and suddenly someone's hand was beneath my shoe – a brief satisfaction in treading down harder, the soft give of those small fingers.

But I couldn't stop, not for a second. I scrambled away from them, only I didn't go the way they thought I would. The classroom door was too closed and too heavy. Besides, I knew that I'd never make it there, between them. They'd never let me through. So I went up instead, up onto a table, and the stacked chairs went tumbling, their metal legs clashing, landing in an awkward spiky pile far below my feet.

"*Run*," said the voices. "Fly."

The windows had been clouded white with condensation. A cut-out paper snowflake wilting from each pane –

I pulled myself up, I pushed my way out.

And then there was that moment when I managed it – when I smashed straight through.

Because suddenly there was the grey sky and a torn paper snowflake and the playground stretching out and out, and there was cold – and for an instant I was safe. I was free. *There was broken glass between us –*

And no way that they could drag me back.

Anna's teacher, I realise, has stopped talking.

She is watching me and waiting and trying not to look like she's wondering anything about me at all.

And, "all right then, Mrs Sawyer," I say to fill in the gap she's left for me.

Her expression barely jumps, but I can tell this wasn't the required response – but what can I do? Her face is so careful it makes me want to laugh out loud. But I mustn't do that. Anna would kill me.

I look around for my daughter, and I find her. She's over in the darkest corner of the playground, near the bins. She's standing so close to her friends that they could be kissing and I stiffen. I don't like it. I watch her hard until she turns and trots back to me, as if I've shouted. *Good girl*, I think. I love her. My little girl –

There's a click. The teacher has slunk back inside. She's closed her heavy door behind her. She'll be keeping her yellow classroom to herself from now on. "*Good*," the voices say.

"Anna," I call as she returns. Just saying it for saying it.

18

Her cheeks are pink, the colour of steamed rhubarb, but I know that if I touched her, she'd feel like ice. She turns and waves to her brown-haired friends.

"See you, Anna!" they shout.

And one of them sends her purple scarf reeling, out, on to the wind. It's a final salute, like semaphore, their particular farewell.

And *my daughter is safe*, I think. It will be all right for her. She's not like me –

"She's like them," the voices say.

"No," I snap. "No, *no*." I'm not listening to that rubbish, no way.

Anna's small cool hand curls around my knuckles. Our fingers tremble together inside my pocket. She rolls her thumb across my scars.

"Hush Mum," she says. "It's OK."

I nod. But of course her palm is freezing, and I snatch my hand away. The other children are all wearing gloves and mittens. I should have bought her gloves.

"*Bad mother*," the voices say. And I cannot disagree.

We walk together to the gate. There's a different crowd there now, I think; it's hard to tell. Certainly, there are more children. They have skin that looks raw and pinched, like Anna's, where the wind has marked them. They are everywhere, these kids, blocking our exit and hanging about, whining, on the pavement outside.

They swing from the blades of their mother's elbows or hang, as if on strings, from their tightly gloved hands. They run and spin and toss their bags towards the clouds or into each other's screeching faces. They make so much noise, unleashing words like weaponry.

"Mum," Anna says, as we sidle closer. "Mum. Please. T-take your hands away from your ears."

She won't look at me. She's ashamed, but what can I do? I can't change. And she knows as well as I do, there are voices.

Berrycake

In the garden, the cat made Gail stop. He was perched high up on the wall above the roses, his eyes unblinking, and she skidded to a halt although she'd hardly covered half the lawn.

Never mind that she'd spent the whole afternoon longing, that she hadn't even waited for the engine to die before leaping from Dad's car, then plunging on, into the house.

Impatiently, she'd stumbled through the party, weaving between men sweating in their suit jackets and women in floral dresses, plucking olives from vintage plates.

"Excuse me," Gail had mumbled. *"Excuse* me..."

At last, managing to tunnel her way free, ducking out through the French windows, shaking off the smoke and perfume and blurring laughter – although not one of those grown-ups had truly noticed *her*, she realised. It was only now, amid the bushes and the birdsong, that she felt seen. The cat's gaze clung to her, eyes like yellow glass.

A ginger Tom. He glowed russet in the sunset, but stepping closer, Gail saw how moth-eaten he was, his ears ragged. He was nothing, no more than a passing stray, and yet she felt suddenly thinned before him, airy. Despite the evening's warmth, she shivered.

She could easily have sent him packing. She could've clapped or shouted or released her own feline hiss – and yet she couldn't even hold his stare. She turned, looking away from the house to the garden, sprawling in the dipping light. Slowly, she took in the

23

buzzing honeysuckle, the rhododendrons with their witches' claws. All she could see of the pond were the lilies, holes torn bright into its darkness. Beyond them, the trampoline's orange had faded to dirty amber – but underneath, Gail knew, her very own Lily would be waiting. She took off once more.

Stupid cat.

He didn't know the garden like Gail did, its scents as green and sweet as limeade that fizzed right through her as she ran – although the garden at dusk was more blue than green, except where flowers like flames split the shadows. Scarlet petals ignited the mauve borders, while the lawn reeled out in neat mown lines, only interrupted by the golden wink of buttercups. It was nothing like Gail's own scrappy backyard; there wasn't a single dandelion here, scarcely a daisy –

She grinned.

And the birds went on calling, unafraid. They didn't care about some stray. Their songs looped and fanned, liquid sounds so that she imagined fountains spraying, taps with beaks. *Chirpy-chirpy, cheep, cheep*, she thought, picturing a radio, her mother; Gail turned her brain off, quick.

At the trampoline, she dropped to her knees and crawled under, between its metal legs.

Inside, the air stank of heated plastic, but it wasn't that that made her gasp, but the way in which the den had been transformed: the picnic rug smoothed across the grass like some magic carpet, the delicate plates loaded and arranged in a tempting spiral. There were candles too, tea-lights, scattered between the crockery like shy little stars.

"Wow," Gail said. "It's just – wow."

Lily giggled, pleased.

24

She was hunched in the reddish shadows on the far side of their spread. She didn't shine like the lilies outside; she was patchier, grubbier, but when she lit the final candle, her eyes flared as yellow as the cat's.

Yet: "You made it then," Lily said, quite human. "Was it horrible in the house? How horrible was it? It's been going on for, like, *forever*. Did they make you talk to them? I could hardly get out. All those questions! It's like... *Spew*."

She raised two fingers to her lips, her soft mouth opening, pretending to gag.

"No one stopped me," Gail replied after a moment. "They didn't even see me."

"God," Lily said. "You're so lucky. They made me play the piano – can you imagine? *Nightmare*."

Gail could imagine.

Lily was wearing the new dress her father had bought her. It was made of stiff cotton, the collar and cuffs indented with stringy vines and pale circles like the holes trapped in a hole-punch. "*Broderie Anglais*," she'd explained the last time that Gail had visited, too many weeks ago. Lily had wrestled it back into her wardrobe, her top lip curling in disgust.

The dress was bunched now into Lily's most ragged pair of jeans, the ones with the lyrics scrawled on them in permanent marker. But where it had come un-tucked, it slid in a heavy white tail behind her and it wasn't hard to picture how it would have looked earlier, falling over the piano stool in waves like cream. Gail thought of Lily's long tanned monkey-toes, bare and brown against the pedals. The entire room sighing as she played.

Trapped at home, Gail would have been sighing then too. Gazing out between the stickers on her bedroom window, waiting for Dad, downstairs, to jingle the car keys. He'd promised her a lift, hours before, but he didn't like her whining. She couldn't ask again.

Gail shook her head. "All this..."

She was struggling to take everything in – the elegant sandwiches, the crackers and cheese, fat strawberries and biscuits, dusted with sugar – the countless cakes. There were gingery wedges and chocolate slices, miniature muffins lurid with frosting, and what looked like a whole uncut Victoria sponge. Thankfully, there weren't any olives though; Gail didn't like olives.

"All for us!" Lily said. "Who needs *them* and their party?" She giggled again and her teeth flashed wickedly. "Just wait until you taste the tea!"

"Tea?"

They'd never had real tea under the trampoline before, as they'd never had real food there either, although there had been summers and summers of hidden picnics. Gail had worried that they wouldn't happen this year, now that they were suddenly so much older, in High School, and in different classes too.

But despite the cat, the way he'd stared, the trampoline enclosed them just as it always had, their rubbery roof floating like some vast dinghy overhead. Lily selected two elfin cups and Gail was stupidly pleased to see that she was using her same old kiddies' tea-set.

Lily lifted the dwarf teapot. "Shall I be Mother?" she cooed.

They laughed.

"Well, you're not a bird," Gail said and Lily laughed harder, the strange cloudy liquid wobbling as she poured.

You're not a bird, Lily Philips – it was a favourite phrase of theirs, first uttered by Lily's stepmother, Eloise, when she'd violated their den three, possibly four years previously. Back when the food wasn't real, when they'd layered the stunted crockery with velvety petals and feathery grasses, with the satisfying crunch of curled-up leaves. But it was the berries that they'd gathered then that had caused Eloise to trespass.

Lily's stepmother had stooped between the struts, perspiration prickling her forehead. When she'd pushed in further, her flustered face had become garish, caught in the trampoline's orange glow.

"I don't usually mind what you and your friends do, Lily. But I saw you at the bush. You can't have those berries under here. You can't play with them. They're poison. Wash your hands."

Lily had shrugged and then quite deliberately reached out to pinch a single berry from their collection. She'd rolled it between her palms, round and round, polishing it until its waxy coating shone.

"I think you've forgotten the rules, *Mother*," Lily had said. "This is one of my Spaces. You aren't allowed here... And besides, the birds eat these berries all the time. I've seen them."

But before Lily had finished speaking, Eloise was already retreating, snatching up the berry bowl as if she thought they'd fight her for it, and: "You're not a bird, Lily Philips!" she cried. Then, bounced back on to the lawn, with only her slim tanned legs revealed to them, she'd said it again: "You're *not* a bird."

And Lily had flicked her solitary berry after Eloise's heels, before catching Gail's eye and collapsing into giggles – just as she giggled now, brandishing their slopping cups.

"It's proper Drink!" she announced. "I raided their glasses. There's wine in there and Champers. Gin too, I think. *Cocktail!*"

Lily downed hers in one and then managed to smack her plump lips even as she shuddered. But when Gail raised her own cup, she ended up coughing, her throat blazing.

"It's like kitchen cleaner," she spluttered, but Lily was already pouring more.

"Drink up!" she said. "Daisy spotted me when I was nicking it, but she knows better than to say anything. Or she'd better know better, anyway. Did you see her in the house? She's been hopping about in her bloody fairy wings all ruddy-bloody afternoon. You know – sucking up to everyone. The little creep."

She did the gag-thing with her fingers again and before Gail knew it, she'd drained her second 'tea', although she was starting to feel genuinely sick herself. Nevertheless, she lifted her empty cup.

"Good girl!" Lily beamed, wielding her teapot. And then: "So, did you? See her?"

Gail began to shake her head, but then remembered: *fairy wings.* Bubble-gum pink, but drooping, overloaded by their sequins and purple feathered trim. Among all those suited men and flowery women, she had, after all, seen Daisy –

Hoisted in her mother's arms, Daisy had appeared clamped to Eloise. At six years old, she was becoming too big to be easily carried. Those wings had sagged from her back, a giant dead moth.

28

Gail's stomach squeezed, a pang of guilt. She ought to have paid more attention. Lily wanted reports; she hated her half-sister as much as she hated her stepmother. *Daisy* – blatantly an inferior flower.

Reading Gail's mind, *"God!"* Lily said. "The Weed's been driving me nuts. As-per-usual. Flitting about, doing her cute act and not one of them sees through it. She's asked for piano lessons too – can you believe it?"

Gail grimaced in sympathy, but Lily wasn't looking. As she reached past to grab a fistful of sandwiches, the alcohol stink doubled, but there was also her own particular Lily-scent, her citrus shampoo and something equally as sweet, but earthier. A pinkish sliver, salmon or ham, dropped from between her fingers.

"Hey," she said, her mouth full. "D'you remember her funeral?"

Of course Gail remembered, although it was years ago, when Daisy was a toddler – one of their first summers of plotting beneath the trampoline. In preparation, they had made Daisy lie down naked on the lawn and then criss-crossed her chubby seal-body with twigs and pebbles.

By the time that they were caught, the trench that they had dug for her was over a foot deep.

"That hole was massive," Gail murmured.

Lily's grin glittered. "Eat," she said.

Gail grabbed a sandwich from the same plate as Lily, but when she took a bite, the butter tasted rancid. The trampoline-air had become oven-like. Gail peered through it, out to where the night was folding in, but the candlelight obscured the garden now and she could only imagine the dark breezes skimming the pond, the clean, cold lilies.

"And then there was Bluebeard..." Lily said.

Gail nodded, recalling how they'd spent hours over that library book, their favourite illustration a row of pretty severed heads.

"Daisy was all the wives," Gail said.

"Oh, yes!" Lily replied. "We were going to dice her!"

She picked up a knife from the cheese plate. It wasn't a tea-set-sized knife, but heavy-duty, swiped from Eloise's kitchen.

"Chop! Chop! Chop!" Lily sang, sweeping the blade through the cloying air before plunging it into the heart of the sponge cake. "We were going to cut her right up! Into little Daisy pieces!"

She handed Gail a slice and more 'tea' and Gail remembered how they'd stripped Daisy that time too, dividing her soft limbs into squares with red felt-tip, imitating the cow diagram at the butcher's.

Queasily, she forced herself to nibble at her cake.

"And do you remember what we did to her when we caught her under here?"

"I do," Gail said, but as Lily chattered on, she found herself drifting. No one, she thought, had ever understood about her and Lily.

Certainly not Gail's parents, who'd never liked Lily ("That posh bint," her father said, while her mother was more cautious, "watch yourself, Kiddo,") and not Lily's new horse-riding friends either, India and Isabella, who rolled their eyes and snorted whenever Gail passed them during school...

And Gail thought about how she'd planned to talk to Lily this evening, about all this, or at least about some of it, about parents, school, those other girls – but perhaps none of that truly mattered? *All for us*, Lily had said – and there was the trampoline still, and the garden. The garden knew –

Just as Gail knew.

That despite its piano and parties and award-winning roses, there was something wrong in Lily's home. The radio never blared too cheerfully there, the way it did at Gail's. The doors didn't slam and nothing ever got smashed and yet from her very first visit it seemed, Gail had sensed how things were for Lily. She couldn't explain – but maybe she didn't have to?

As Lily went on recounting their endless tales – the tripwires, and the frog in Daisy's cot, the bucket balanced on the nursery door – Gail knew that no matter what else India and Isabella might offer, they'd never understand about Daisy. Not like she did.

As if to confirm it, Lily broke off mid-sentence. She bit her lip.

"It's only getting worse," she whispered. "The way that Daisy is with Dad. With how she's changing him."

"Oh, Lily."

Gail inched closer, but her stomach tipped. Her head wasn't right either. It felt tight and greasy, because of the heat or the 'tea', possibly both. But Lily looked just the same; she went on shimmering, mottled with gold from the candlelight, her blond head bowed –

And suddenly Gail found herself transfixed by the embroidery on Lily's dress – momentarily consumed by the urge to press her fingertips into those cut-out discs, to trace the stitching that draped her collar-bones, the tiny spying buttons at her neck. They were pearls, those buttons, and there was something pearly

31

glistening through the air between them too – Lily's sadness, that only Gail had ever glimpsed. It swirled like the patterns in smoked glass.

Gail longed to reach out, but a wave of shyness found her peeping back out towards the garden. Darkness lapped between the trampoline's legs, an indigo tide, and she was suddenly filled with a renewed urge to speak. She wanted to tell Lily how magical everything remained, how genuinely beautiful –

But there was a bang, a clatter of doors, voices escaping from the house. Eloise's voice slashing through the rest: "Lily! Lily, Love – where are you? We're about to cut Dad's cake!"

"Shit," Lily said, scrubbing at her face. "They'll want the knife."

She rose and then having forgotten their trampoline-ceiling, staggered back on to her knees. She crawled past, away from Gail, trailing her lemony scent and her unravelling dress.

"Lily," Gail said.

"Be back..." Lily slurred.

From the edge of the trampoline, Gail watched Lily race through the shadows towards the house. The night wasn't as deep as she'd thought; the summer evening was undercut with swathes of light and the air retained its silkiness – and yet there were stars. They plinked through the softness like Lily's piano notes, putting their picnic candles to shame.

Beneath those stars, Lily grew smaller. But as she zigzagged across the silvery lawn, the knife flashed, caught in the glare from the French windows, and Gail felt a thrill running up her own arms. A hot sweet shiver in her chest.

Back in the house, they still didn't see her. Gail felt as if she was in a dream, someone else's dream – Lily's, probably. She was practically swaying and yet it was easy to slip past the couples in the hall, to pad up the stairs, to find the right room.

The door had been left ajar. There was a nightlight burning in one corner and a mobile hanging from the ceiling that at first she took to be lilies, more lilies, but was actually a drift of paper swans.

Gail stumbled on, towards the bed.

"Daisy," she whispered.

Daisy rolled over in the fuzzy dim, her hair like fur against the pillow. Her eyelids flickered. Downstairs, they were singing.

"*Happy Birthday to you!*"

But Daisy didn't wake.

Gail bent over her, close enough to smell her cotton bedclothes, to make out the wings, still strapped to her, pulled roughly on over her pyjamas. The wings dragged at Daisy's flannel collar and although they were bent, half-crushed, beneath her, they looked larger than before, a looming stain across the sheet.

But as Gail stood there, trembling despite the night's warmth, she found herself focusing with a strange sharp clarity. Tracing the wings' feathered frills and winking sequins as if she'd acquired a cat's night-vision –

The cat, Gail realised, was back.

Somehow, it had followed her inside, or else pre-empted her. It was crouched on Daisy's wardrobe, another patch of deeper dark, only the yellow of its eyes giving it away. And maybe, Gail wondered, it was the cat who'd dreamt her here?

Downstairs, the singing stopped and just before the entire house awoke, erupting with cheers, the stray stretched, its shadowy shape elongating, and yet still, it didn't blink. It held Gail steadily in its cool, glass gaze, staring down at what she was holding –

At the cake that she had made so very special for Lily's little sister – a cake jewelled as generously as those fairy wings, its icing heaped with plucked red beads.

The Dining Room Ghost

Every night, the woman is there. Every single night, as you follow the crooked Victorian steps that wind down from the nursery, with the baby hot and heavy on your shoulder, you know that she will be there, waiting.

She is always in the same place, in the dining room. She keeps to her own particular corner, hovering with the shadows beside the ticking Grandmother clock that came with the bricks and mortar.

"Another period feature," you tell your husband, when he phones.

Always, she stands in that same grey spot, with her head bowed and her shoulders hunched, her hands knotted at her thighs. Beneath her long dress, her feet are bare and stained. Between the dirt that strings up from her soles like seaweed, her anklebones shine. They are so pale as to be almost blue. Her toenails glint like broken glass.

Her feet are her most distinctive feature. The patches through the grime are the only sections of her skin that you can see clearly. Her tangled hands are sketchy, roped against her cloud-like dress, and because of the way in which her head droops, you have never once yet seen her face.

For many nights, you have dreaded that. That moment when her head will rise, when finally you'll feel her gaze on yours. You have dreaded it so sharply, so repeatedly, that at times the fear has twisted, as a blade might, and:

Get it over with, you think then. *Just get it done...*

Although perhaps, it is simply because her hair is so unnerving? While she holds the rest of herself so perfectly still, those hanging curls hint at motion, so that you find yourself imagining giant lice and squirming beetles, a darker flicker between the tangles. If you were able to hear them, those creatures would click and whisper; they'd rustle like bin-bags. Like the things that you might find in bin-bags, scuttling rot. Sometimes you feel the itch of them on your own scalp, their countless catching furry legs...

Every night, counting down those steps – *thirteen, twelve, eleven, ten* – you see the woman even before you've reached the dining room. You're already picturing her as you concentrate, descending oh-so-carefully, because the staircase is so steep and narrow. The house's spine, as chilly as bone, it aches with its age beneath your own bare feet.

And of course you also tread cautiously because your arms are full. As your head is full, with the baby. You have no spare hand to clutch at the banister. Scarcely a gap for proper thought around his crying.

If the woman in the dining room were to make any sound at all, you'd never hear it, although by step four or step three, even while you're focusing on that final splintered corner, you can smell her.

Her scent is powerful, both beautiful and repugnant. It is smoke and it is autumn. She is the mulch that hides beneath the golden fall of leaves, and she is carbon. She is pink match-heads scorched to black and the cold hollow of a long-dead hearth. She is the ashes there, piled in cobwebbed layers, as fine and feathery as lace.

The woman smells of everything that your baby doesn't. As he reels against your breasts, he is all hot, dreaming flesh and wet towelling. Thrumming with such ferocious beating life –

Nevertheless, you can imagine how very easily his scents might be consumed by hers. Lapping over the pair of you, in a sooty tide...

"Well, at least you have company," your husband tells you. His voice, kept deliberately light, creeps, tentative, through the crackle on the line.

"But never for long."

You have tried to explain how quickly your ghost can vanish, fluttering out like ancient celluloid, scratching back into the wall's dim grain. And how her disappearing can at times be as disturbing as her presence.

And yet you laugh into the receiver as if you are not scared. It's an odd sort of laughter though, giddy and gulped, and with the long-distance, you hear it echoing back at you, your giggles transformed into something strange, a stranger's laughter. It's as if there is another woman – *yet* another woman – trapped amid the static, or else holed up even further away, in your husband's hotel room... Isn't it possible that he has company of his own?

Lately, when you reach the dining room, you've pretended to ignore your waiting ghost – as you pretend that what you're doing downstairs is soothing your frantic, screaming son. The hard chill of the dark-lacquered parquet is undeniable; it rises up through your soles, so much less giving than the creaking steps – and yet you walk single-mindedly across the room.

You turn on the stereo, attempting to swamp the crying, or to at least locate some different rhythm underneath it. And while you do so, you no longer look directly towards the Grandmother clock, but only hold that corner of the room in the corner of your eye. In that manner, you're sometimes able to keep the woman, to contain her. You'd rather know exactly where she is. Clutching the baby, and fumbling your steps as you attempt to dance, you have feared her flying at you, unreeling like some devil in a horror film, attacking –

But as your son battles against you, his crying intensifying, you wonder if it's the woman who is angry.

Before the baby was born, when you first came to live in this house, this most desirable of properties, so different from the Lego-like rooms where you grew up, the woman wasn't there. Or if she was, you couldn't see her, as your husband still can't see her on his fleeting visits between work.

Back then, in the summer, every elegant room, every corner, had been dappled with light. Dust-motes swam like cotton-fluff and twinkled as they turned, and wherever shadows did manage to fall, they were gentle things, velvety, laden with hope as your body was laden. Tingling with your life, and more.

It is a struggle to conjure that time back now. To believe in it. The house then, so sensuous around you, and how you drifted through it, safe in your proud, growing body, your shared body, all of it carried so carefully. That August warmth.

It is difficult, now that your body feels full of blackness, now that there is nothing but black in that space where the baby isn't any longer. Even as he was being born, you seemed to sense it pouring through you. A clumped emptiness rushing to fill that gap. It makes no sense, and yet...

So strongly had you felt it that you'd expected the blood that seeped out of you to be black too, blacker than mud. Instead, it was scarlet – crimson! As bright as a balloon. It had surprised you as your milk continues to surprise you, with its pallor. It creeps out of you as you dance, this milk that the baby wants so furiously, so feverishly, but fights to drink. It stains the baggy T-shirt that you wear to sleep in. It leaves white, wilting petals on all of your clothes.

You first glimpsed your ghost on the night when you returned from the hospital, your son just four days old. There she was, in her corner, a streak of cold, of frozen time, beside the clock's tick-tock. She was exactly the same then, as now – that matted hair, those glassy feet.

You didn't scream that first night, but you did flee, clumsily, colliding back up the twisted steps, back to your bedroom, to where your husband had been then, sleeping. You woke him: "There's a woman," you said. "A ghost downstairs – "

Yet practically right away, you'd found yourself smiling, instinctively returning your husband's bleary grin, his shaking head. It was ludicrous; you both knew it. Especially coming from you, when you'd always been the clear-minded one, bold – pushing for this beautiful house, and then pushing for the pregnancy. Always knowing exactly what you wanted and then making it happen.

"It's sleep deprivation," your husband had said. "Escaping dreams..."

And as you'd nodded, he had reached across the covers, eased the wriggling baby from the clamp of your arms.

"Poor thing," he said. "Poor frightened thing."

Except the next night, of course the woman had been there again, and the next, and despite your fear, as whole months have passed, you have come to study her. She remains dreadful, but you're fascinated. Her pristine stillness, her precarious bones –

Inside the smudged hang of her dress, she is scarecrow-thin, and you have considered the possibility that she isn't a ghost after all, but a witch.

"Or perhaps some kind of combination? A witch-ghost?" you suggested to your husband, yesterday evening, when he called. And then you tried not to hear his replying sigh.

It has seemed natural, essential even, the way in which the woman has become such a long-standing joke, except that maybe by now, the joke is wearing through? Becoming a tired story like the others you recite – tales about rambling strolls in the bare treed park and the support of parent groups, and happiness.

Far away, your husband sighs, and again and again, you hear your own strange laugh, and nothing changes. The baby cries. The woman waits.

You do not share her patience.

As you dance your ridiculous dining-room-dance, clenching your son tighter when he heats and buckles – as the crying continues, impossibly, on and on – it strikes you.

Perhaps she isn't patient, perhaps she isn't waiting? Maybe, for all these nights, it has been you?

You, who has felt the dread warp, twisting into anticipation. You, in this dining room, sensing hunger. Your own hunger, you realise – your eagerness. For the woman to look up, to see you. For the connection to be made.

With your fingers scrabbling around your squalling son, you understand.

Get it over with. Just get it done...

And at last, you can imagine it, so cleanly, so clearly: how you will set your sadness down, and how in exchange, you might be granted silence.

You think of this house, without the telephone ringing. And free of your own laughter, free of his screaming.

This is what *you* have been longing for. Her silence wrapped about you, as soft as fog.

You can feel how close it is. So close, you see it happen.

Your damp hands opening, the letting go –

The baby finally lying still, before her dirty, shining feet.

Coach Trip

Anita was plummeting.

Plummeting in a rattling coach through Europe's second longest land tunnel. She had no idea how long they'd been inside, but it was a long, long time, that was for sure.

Long, she thought. *L-o-o-o-n-g.*

The word itself was like a yawn; she wished that she could crash, badly, but while she might have been dozing (her thoughts flickered with red strings and ashes, some impatiently waiting dream), she knew she wouldn't be able to drop off completely. The teachers had given up hours back, and even without the snide murmurs and blatant laughter coming from Louise's friends, there were too many other idiots on board.

They were all over the place, lobbing Coke cans and crisp packets, swinging ape-like between the seats. They squawked and chattered like primates too, *gibbering like gibbons*; the static-flecked movie playing on the screen above the driver might as well have been switched to 'mute'.

And the coach was way too hot, as well. Before entering the tunnel, they'd been instructed in no uncertain terms to snap the windows closed. This was, after all, Europe's second longest land-tunnel – that had to mean some *serious* fumes.

Turning her back, not just on Louise, but on the entire squalling-squealing coach, Anita pressed her forehead to the juddering glass. It was still lukewarm, not cool like she'd anticipated, and for perhaps the hundredth (thousandth, millionth?) time, she attempted to focus only on the concrete pouring past, the orange lights. They were an oily kind of orange. *Greasy* – as if their glow had somehow trapped the petrol stink that the panes cut out. And the walls were gritty, harsh; it was like plunging into some man-made tank, a brutal aquarium, drained of water.

Drained of fish too...

And there was nothing fluid about how the coach battered along (*long*). Against the window, Anita could feel the engine's jolts running from her teeth to the clicking hinges of her jaw – and how skull-like her reflection appeared! She was all sockets and hollows and withering lines, although the tunnel's bulbs made her gleam amber rather than white. She'd grown a pumpkin-face, as if it was Halloween –

Witch, that's what Louise's friends called Anita. *Witch-bitch* –

That's what they'd written on the balled-up note, thrown at her head as soon as the lighting had changed, when they'd first entered the tunnel. The note had bounced with a sickening softness from Anita's shoulder to her lap. It lay there, still.

But she mustn't think about the note or Louise, or witches, none of that. Somewhere high, high, overhead, she knew there was a true white, far better than bone or screwed-up paper. There was snow – mountains. Giant versions of the Toblerone bars that had been stacked in every shop since leaving the ferry – the *white* chocolate variety, obviously. Anita pictured their looming chunks, but not quite the blue that they'd be pressed against. That would be clearer and cleaner, far more pure and perfect than anything she could currently imagine. Maybe it didn't exist?

No more sky, Anita thought.

And then: *how long had they been in this stupid tunnel?*

Without meaning to, she'd withdrawn from the glass. It took a moment to register the sucking-kissing sound that her skin made as it unglued, and several further seconds to notice the smear that her forehead had left there. It seemed to collect, like smoke, only after she'd pulled away. *Time's gone squiffy*, she thought. The whole holiday was wrong.

A Year Ten combined Art-History trip to Italy. Two weeks of golden coliseums and echoing galleries. Charcoal smudging with suntan-cream as they sketched... That's how Anita's mother would be envisioning it, anyway.

"But Darling! It's such an opportunity!" she'd cried, plucking the letter from the dumped debris of Anita's schoolbag. "You really *must* go!"

Aside from failing to consider the time spent driving from London, two whole days inside this coach even before reaching the tunnel – the sheer *length* of that – Anita's mother was clueless about Louise.

There was no way that Anita had been able to confess how things had changed between them, not when she could barely explain it to herself. And it wasn't just that they'd been Best Friends Forever (or so she'd thought), their mothers got on brilliantly too; they'd be distraught if they learnt the truth. Anita imagined them, vividly, clinging to one another and *wailing*, acting like their girls had died or something...

On the screen, the movie fluttered, fading in and out. One of the boys near the front rolled, grinning, into the aisle. His friends whooped – *howler monkeys.* Pointedly, Anita turned her attention to the film. Or pretended to. She'd seen it before.

49

It was one of those rainy Sunday afternoon things, made for watching far from here, curled up in the safe boredom of her bedroom, eating cold pizza with the curtains drawn. A black-and-white tale of misunderstanding and murder and well-cut suits. Even without being able to hear, Anita knew what was happening; the main characters, both men, were seated at a table on a train (yet more travelling!), the slightly baggier man proposing that they swapped killings, a hated father for a hated wife. The younger, handsome actor laughing, assuming (fatally, of course) that it was all one big joke.

This particular scene was more familiar than Anita had first realised – not just from home, hadn't it played on this journey already? Maybe the film had come to an end and looped back? Briefly, she wondered if she'd actually slept after all – except that then the static that had been edging the movie erupted, forming a total *snowstorm*, consuming the picture entirely. A heartbeat later, the screen turned black.

When it wavered back to life, the monochrome suited men had vanished, replaced by a serious young woman in full colour, wearing a slickly sleeveless blouse. A news report, although it wasn't a local channel, but Sky (Sky, of course! Unashamedly sky-less) and Anita didn't know how *that* worked. Was it possible to get reception this far underground?

The picture flashed from the woman to footage of a roadside. Dark tarmac and rocks like large spilt teeth, fuzzily discernible behind wasp-bright police tape and the chilly blue sweep of emergency lights. A tagline ran across the screen – *BREAKING STORY* – and Anita thought about that, about how stories might break. She was somewhat relieved that the movie had cut out.

50

She wasn't sure that she liked the film's message –
the first murder happened, and so another was expected
– a few offhand remarks and you're doomed; your life
no longer under your control.

Anita thought about the conversations she'd had,
months ago, with Louise, winding her up about her new
haircut and her eyeliner – the casual jibes she'd
directed at Billy too.

Stupid, Anita thought now, how she'd blathered
on, but then how was she meant to have known?
Louise had giggled right alongside her, and they'd
always teased one other. It was how they *were*
together. On the same page...

Obviously not.

Surreptitiously, Anita lowered her gaze to her lap
to scan the hurled note, reading it again.

Witch-bitch!
Wierdo!
Freakoid!!!
Lezzer!

A rainbow-coloured list, each line glittered with
the eager ink of a different gel-pen. The handwriting
differed too, none of it actually Louise's, but Anita
didn't try to kid herself about that. The enthusiastically
bubbled 'i's and exclamation marks belonged to the
girls who Louise hung out with now, her new loyal
crew – girls that they'd previously disdained because of
their dead-straightened hair and boy-fixations.

Anita could hear them now, crowded four rows
behind, taking up the privileged back seat and
screaming laughter. Did they ever do anything but
scream?

Perspiration licked the nape of Anita's neck, the
coach's scorched air pressing closer, along with their

51

noise. Had Louise's friends realised that she was reading them? *Re*-reading them, over and over –

Wierdo!

Freakoid!!!

Lezzer!

The last, Anita knew, was because she hadn't understood about Billy. About Louise-and-Billy. The boy was a walking brick, as sun-baked and as dense as that – hadn't Anita told Louise that? *Fatally*, it seemed now...

But honestly, if Louise wanted his stumpy builder's hands all over her, then that was her problem, and so it wasn't that, but the witch comments that burnt into Anita. Because the betrayal *there*, sank so much deeper.

When they'd been little girls, careless of their knotted hair and grass-stained jeans, back when the whole world had felt as easily stretched and roll-able as play-dough, Anita and Louise had played The Wishing-Game. They'd played it obsessively.

Holding sweaty hands and whispering, grubby faces clenched in concentration, they'd agreed on the stuff that they'd needed to happen, and there were times, many times, when their wishes appeared to work.

Mostly, it was little things – a connived sleepover or a mother appearing with a freshly baked cake, but there had also been the dull picnic thrown into glorious disarray by a swarm of marauding bees, and once, an entire tray of lumpy custard overturning in the dinner hall. There had even been the hated Year Three teacher who had disappeared on sick leave...

They'd had witchy powers, Anita especially; they'd been convinced of that for years – and perhaps, they'd gone on believing it. Only last summer, when they were supposedly still close ("like sisters!" as their mothers shrilled), Louise had continued calling on Anita's skills on a daily basis, after school. They had pretended it was nothing, something funny that they'd once shared, but skulking between the Leylandii outside Billy's house, Louise had begged her to will him out.

"C'mon, 'Nita! You're just not wishing hard enough!"

And hadn't Louise got what she'd wanted in the end?

Not just Billy, but sudden boobs – an uplift bra to go with her new haircut, not to mention an entire back row of screaming friends. Whereas Anita...

Maybe she thought she'd used up all the magic for Louise? Or perhaps, in a weird way, she'd grown (yet more) superstitious? Perhaps she was scared to want things now – hadn't she secretly believed that there'd be a price to pay, one day, for all those wishes coming true? Maybe Anita was paying that price, right now? Paying it endlessly? Repeatedly –

Except, if she was honest, the wishing-habit hadn't truly left her. It was too ingrained. Anita felt the urge sometimes as a sort of electricity, wishes simmering and sparking beneath her skin. Perhaps it was only that her desires lately were too fierce, too fiery, to even be whispered?

There had been moments recently, moments during her bleakest, loneliest, *longest* schooldays, when Anita had found herself picturing her own crowded funeral. Mourners, mothers especially, *wailing*, clad in black – a joint funeral, because Louise too –

No – not ever *that*.

Anita just wanted Louise back. Obviously.

She wanted Louise nearby again, for always. Those new shrieking friends vanished, as if in a puff of smoke. *Razed to the ground –*

But really, she had to stop thinking like this! It would only drive her crazy. Crazier. Especially trapped as she was, her worries circling like some stupid carousel. Besides, for now, right now, her wishes were simple things. And quite normal, surely – she only wanted cool air and an end to this tunnel. Oh, how she wished that she could...

CRASH read the screen's tagline.

The cameras had zoomed in. There was the same sooty road criss-crossed with hazard-stripes, but Anita could see now how the night had thickened with foggy plumes. Beyond the smoke, those boulders like teeth littered the base of some sheer cliff – and within that, there was a deeper darkness. A brutal man-made entrance in the rock, its dank black tinged unnaturally, a sickly orange deepening to red.

The opening was unnerving, and unnervingly familiar, suggestive of a gaping, blood-streaked mouth...

Anita didn't like it; she didn't like it all, but no one else appeared disturbed, or even to be paying attention. The entire coach went on gibbering. One of the boys tumbled from his seat, squaring his mouth like a baboon.

But then the television's white noise returned, noiseless against the coach's roar. The static was a blizzard, *pure snow -*

And somewhere, high, high, overhead, Anita remembered, there were mountains. Giant Toblerones...

Mesmerised, she watched the static whirling, faster and faster, just like her thoughts, and it came to her how the old movie ended, with an actual carousel. A brake-less carousel spinning out of control – she saw it clearly, and not for the first or even the second time, she was certain – two men fighting beneath the wild, painted eyes of wooden horses. Those rhythmic, pounding hooves...

It was a great scene, literally spiralling with tension – but maybe Anita was mistaken? When the film resumed once more, the men were still on their train, having their same conversation –

The movie had definitely gone wonky, the timing screwed. *And how long had they been in this stupid tunnel anyway?*

Anita stretched, exhaustion coating her clammy face and limbs with a second sticky skin. At least her friendlessness allowed her a whole double-seat to herself. Maybe she'd finally sleep? Then she might be able to forget how her head kept pitching, the around-and-around nature of her thinking, and the fact that there remained (that there went on remaining) no sign of any exit, never mind a glimpse of sky... Had she forgotten the sky?

The coach just kept on, battering along, its temperature and screeching rising. A crumpled Coke can soared, shining, into the aisle, and as the tunnel tightened and the light transformed, the baggier man on screen proposed an undetectable crime. The younger handsome actor laughing, as if it was all one big joke –

And suddenly, the only thing Anita longed for was to understand.

She wished –

The coach swerved.

The screen fragmented and she had no idea whether they'd smashed to a halt, or whether they were still flying. Something struck the back of her head – a sickening softness ran from her shoulder to her lap – and then everything flared.

Her dreams, the coach, the entire tunnel –

Orange became black, a suffocating darkness strung with red, and Anita felt the heat and the terror. She heard a shattering, almost sharp enough to drown out the screaming.

Louise –

She didn't know if she'd cried the word aloud. Anita didn't know anything; her heart was on fire.

There was fire – true flames, blazing brighter than wishes. A bloodied mouth engulfing them, rock-teeth closing in, and

Anita was plummeting.

Plummeting in a rattling coach through Europe's second longest land tunnel. She had no idea how long they'd been inside, but it was a long, long time, that was for sure.

Long, she thought. *L-o-o-o-n-g.*

And the word itself was like a yawn;

The Woman Under the Ground

Cara's back in the woods. It's a winter's afternoon like so many afternoons; the sky's white and ragged through the trees. The ground is steeped with leaves, as patched and patterned as charred toast.

At first, she strides ahead as if inspired, inspiring, marching into the cobwebs of her own huffed breath. Mulch clings to her impractical boots and even in her gloves, her pockets, her hands stay cold. The children lag behind.

Every now and then, she turns to them.

While Tammy, Cara's youngest, dodges creeping bushes, the twins stick to the centre of the path, although they're weaving several feet apart. Their shoulders are hunched, chins dipped towards their i-Pods. Ben's bowed head is a crow-black tangle, gold only at the roots. Helen gleams. Brilliantly blond against the sodden greens and mottled browns, the ghostly grey of latticed branches. With the chill, she's already beginning to frizz and ripple, her hair clenching back towards its natural curls.

Headphones firmly plugged in, each immersed in their own distinctly different music, the twins don't look up to find their mother's gaze, and nor to one another. And yet each child sways in rhythm, as if they're two parts of the same. It is how they've always been, despite Ben's crude dye, despite Helen's straighteners. Irretrievably connected.

Tammy catches up, abruptly bundling between them. She arrives muttering, mid-sentence. Wondering about the dead-leaf crunch, and about her wellies, their blue and yellow polka dots. Yet after a moment, *she* remembers Cara.

She inclines her head, and there's that softness to her eyes. *Tammy's eyes...* As always, Cara resists the urge to turn away.

After all, her littlest is waving, although with her next clumsy step, Tammy's already distracted. Bowing with concern over some peeling twig or pearly pebble. Tucked too tightly into her padded coat, her hair hangs in pallid lines and Cara catches herself picturing thin, poured tea. *Lukewarm*, she thinks.

She shifts her attention back to her own feet, to her preposterous boots with their mud-sticking heels and cracks and streaks. They're her oldest pair. These days, this is the only place she would think to wear them, although the worn leather goes on cradling her calves like appreciative hands, and they remain, insistently, beautiful. *Those stains...*

In a kind of daze, as if they don't belong to her, Cara watches her rumpled feet negotiate knotted roots and mossy rocks. The gentle parting of the leaves.

She refuses to look up, to glance ahead, to the place where the path is pulling them. She doesn't even want to breathe the forest down too deeply. *Not yet.* She ought to savour it all, slowly – this walk, these unfolding woods, this perfect, paling afternoon. At the same time of course, she can't face any of it. It's all too tangled – *not yet, please.*

But the trees press close and the scents accost her, regardless. Musky bark and the acrid odour of snapped bracken, and that taste like yellowed metal to the air. Most of all, there's the curious sweetness of the dark earth that's packed beneath her. Before her.

It's irresistible. One of the main reasons why she's back here, why today, with the weather like this, she couldn't prevent herself from returning. The same way she wears these tired, beloved boots because –

Because.

Cara stops in her tracks.

And then listens to her own voice, surprisingly harsh.

"Come on, you lot! Get a move on."

In truth, attempting to rouse herself, to remind herself.

Don't be sad, Cara. Don't be sad.

"You know you'll love it when you get there," she'd told the twins before they left.

And although it has been years, it's true, they do.

When Cara stops walking, her children take over. It isn't long before Ben's bounding ahead, leaping a slick, black stump, loose bootlaces whirling, and there's a new lightness to Helen's step too that she can't disguise. At the very beginning, before anything else, this place was theirs, although they'd never acknowledge it. Nevertheless, they know exactly where they're heading.

Only Tammy goes on dawdling. Her commentary has grown slightly desperate, sharpening to a sing-song chirrup as she continues to search, to treasure-hunt. Cara waits for her to take off again before following.

Already, the twins have vanished, flitting between the sudden firs where the path twists and forks. Beneath her scarf, Cara can feel her pulse. A fragile ticking in her throat –

Already, they'll have found the woman. Their own rediscovery.

61

Yet it's only now that Cara fully allows herself to draw down the day. She fills her lungs with woolly damp, and with each blink uncovers a new pattern in the bark. Bold lines and inky webs, unfathomable words.

She lets the trees surround her.

High above, in a hole between the netted branches, there's a tiny plane. So distant, it appears suspended, hardly moving. A paper cut-out on the smoky sky. And Cara remembers how, way before Tammy, before these woods meant anything much, she used to watch the planes. How when they first moved here, she'd feel herself shift inside with the turn of their wings. Her longing unreeling with their fleecy tails as she waited for Mark, her husband, to come home.

Back then, when she'd believed in something perfect, or at least, a striving for perfection, she'd celebrated each of his returns with a feast. A succulent joint, slow-simmering in the oven, further complicated dishes on the stove. She'd wanted a house suffused with the welcoming scents of browning meat and melting butter. She'd wanted candlelight, and peace. Although inevitably, one course or another would burn and the twins would fuss, becoming fractious, sent to bed on time, for once.

And even then, Mark too would never be quite what she'd envisaged. Despite his catnap, jetlag would shade his features like the rub of grubby fingers. His mouth tightening with the effort of it all, while Cara often spent far too long with her clanking pans, her own face straining. Staining. Mascara bruising, and sometimes running, with the steam.

And later of course, it was the planes taking off that had caused her heart to twist. The space without Mark, and what that could mean.

Eagerly in front now, Tammy wades between the pine needles, following her siblings through the gap into the clearing, and Cara comes up quickly behind her. Faster than she'd intended. So fast that with a rush like gulped breath, it is upon her.
This place.
J –

His unfamiliar fingers curled around hers. The novelty of holding hands, because they could out here. Because Mark was far away, and there wasn't another soul about to see them.

Although for a while, she'd remained shy with him, snatching glances, even with his thumb circling her palm. Even as the ripples shuddered through her. It was insanity how much she'd wanted him. The stroke of his coat hem sweeping her thigh –

Impatiently, Cara pushes through the clinging branches. She only remembers to duck at the very last moment and ends up staggering, as clumsy as Tammy. She practically falls into the clearing, and it isn't good enough. Because her twins are waiting. And the woman.

Helen and Ben had been no bigger than Tammy when they'd found her. It was back in that before-time, during those early, waiting, plane-watching days, when it had just been the three of them, walking together. Until that afternoon when the two of them had streaked off in a whole new direction. Soaring, as if called. But before Cara had had time to unpick her panic, they were calling out to her. Not lost at all, simply high-pitched and excited from beyond the blue fir boughs.

"There's a woman, Mummy! *Come and see.* A woman under the ground."

She hadn't hurried. The twins' lives then had been fraught with tiny, bright discoveries. Their delight and terror as intently felt, and as easily plucked, as their splinters. Generally, Cara had attended to them in a daze, wavering between busyness and exhaustion. In some way or another, she'd always struggled to keep up.

And it had been such a fine spring afternoon when they'd come across their woman, winter swept away. Lifting those heavy branches, Cara had let herself be distracted by their fringes, and by the birdsong. By the idea of all those tight little buds on the brink of unfolding. The air was rich and ripe, tinged green, and Cara's stomach had stirred with a blend of happiness and hunger. And it was the light that had struck her first, before her children, or even the woman there. She can picture it, still, *so beautiful –*

The way it had fallen, slicing through the branches. Gold columns hanging like smoke between that green. Turning like water, each one tumbling with flecks, with seeds or pollen. *Tiny sea-beings, aglitter.*

Cara's children had been similarly dappled – while the woman spread-eagled at the heart of the clearing was barred with light, strapped down by it. As if it wasn't quite enough that she was under the ground, she had needed binding too.

Smiling, Cara had walked over to her, and to the twins huddled at her side. All big eyes and open mouths, so dazzlingly gilded in that moment, she'd had to blink away. *Miraculous creatures…*

"It's all right," she'd told them.

Because of course the woman wasn't really a woman.

"It's just earth," Cara had said, wondering aloud about underlying rocks and lumpen roots. The freakishness of nature. Yet that sprawled shape remained incredible, despite her reasoning – and so perfectly centred beneath the trees. Even the nettles crowded a respectful distance back.

When Cara had drawn closer, the mounds that might have been a head and two firm breasts only grew more definite, and it had made her laugh. Nothing but bumped, slumped soil. And yet so distinctly, unnervingly, a woman.

It wasn't just her breasts and the embedded rise and sink of her shoulders, there were also furrows that seemed to suggest the length of her arms, and a pair of strong legs. A possible dip between her dusty thighs.

Although she lay larger than any human woman, it was astonishing how properly proportioned she'd appeared, so that briefly Cara had wondered if she wasn't in fact man-made? The work of some secretive artist? But the thought was easily dismissed: the figure was somehow too much a part of these woods to have been imagined elsewhere; she'd grown *here*.

Yet nothing grew on her, Cara had realised. And that was strange.

The twins had listened to her explanations, the possibilities, their faces dubious. They didn't ask a single question. Once Cara's reassurances were over, all Helen said was: "We're keeping her," and Ben had nodded. "She's our lady now."

And so it was decided. After that, they had to keep coming, back and back. It became a weekly occurrence, at least. At some point, one of them declared the woman a sacrifice – they were probably at school by then, investigating Aztecs – while the other determined that she was definitely alive under there, only sleeping, waiting, just like them.

They took it in turns with their stories and occasionally, they'd pounced on her, throwing rocks and stabbing her with sticks. Kicking up her powder while their eyes flashed and their cheeks blazed, their laughter like screaming, ecstatic and appalled. Such frenzies never lasted long though, and mostly, they fell hushed before her. They had started leaving gifts.

Snail shells and bracelets of petals, gleaming bone-like stones. One summer's day, a three foot-long daisy chain that Helen had been meticulously winding since the house. The offerings, the visits, rapidly became ingrained. Such a part of their routine that when Cara had finally returned to the woods without her children, she couldn't seem to prevent her feet, these boots, from leading the same way. She hadn't meant to –

But until Tammy arrived and Mark stopped travelling, until these last few years when the house had closed in, she'd kept returning.

With J.

As if there was nowhere else for them to go.

There wasn't any wind, that first time. No real rain either, just chilly damp, the air silvery with moisture. But Cara had been warm inside her boots. And shivery-hot wherever he touched her. His fingers on her neck, even before they'd kissed –

On the way, he had put her hand inside his pocket and she'd felt him. Laughing clumsily, a thin gasping, made stupid with desire.

They'd intended to lay down their coats, but in the end, there wasn't time. She'd had to pull off her boots though, one at least, in order to peel free her woollen tights, her underwear – the absurdity of clothes. She'd fumbled with the leather, and when she finally managed to grasp the zip, the sound of its teeth unhooking had made her wince. Like ripping a plaster from a weeping knee. A brutal noise, beside the quiet. Their breath –

"Who's that, Mummy?"

Tammy.

Cara drags herself back.

Of course the woman's still there. Where else could *she* go?

For a moment, Cara's old smile appears. A brief, ghost smile. Even though the woman's grey this afternoon, soft and exhausted-looking and perhaps not quite as big as Cara remembered.

And yet her figure remains unmistakable. Rough head, those breasts, the reaching paw-like hands. Slowly, heavily, Cara lifts her gaze to Helen, and then Ben.

But the twins no longer seem interested in their lady, their rituals. They stand a little way off, beside the holly. Helen's tugging the headphones from her ears, but she doesn't glance over. Neither of them do.

And even Tammy's trudging off again now, already distracted by a paper-lined cone or an acorn cup, woodlice.

So Cara's alone as she approaches. Transfixed as she recalls the dreams she used to have about this

67

woman, night after night, once she'd stopped visiting. Dreams of digging, of clawing … And she remembers too how whenever she left this clearing – not with Mark, never with Mark, but with J – she'd always glance back, a grin running right through her as she nodded goodbye.

Thank you, that's what she used to think. As if the woman was their secret keeper. As if she could keep them safe.

Sometimes, afterwards, they would go for a drink, J and Cara. Knocking back whiskies in some dozy pub, high and thirsty and relieved. Just once, they went to a café in the furthest village instead, where Cara had giggled at the Battenburg. At the unreality of it all.

She'd been in such a haze that afternoon, so stunned still, looking back at him, that by the time she brought the rimmed china to her mouth, her tea had cooled; it was almost undrinkable. And with that lukewarm sip, came the realisation of time. Of endings. How they were always leaving one other.

"Don't be sad," he had told her. "Don't be sad."

His eyes tugging at Cara as she gathered up her purse and brushed viciously at her boots. Practical measures to hold back a terrible, swooping vision of her golden twins waiting. Just the two of them waiting, in that wide, grey playground, at the end of school.

Hopeless, Cara thinks now.

Stupid.

Stupid to have come back here. And to have brought the kids with her –

She can hardly look at the woman anymore. That woman made of dirt.

68

At the clearing's edge, the undergrowth ripples, scuffles. There are creatures hiding there, furtive, scratching things. The bushes flounce with their squabbling, while overhead the branches shift, just perceptibly, with the wind. They remain stiff against the white, while far beyond them, another plane…

My children, Cara thinks.

Turning her attention back to Helen, who's leaning towards her brother now, untangling him, fitting her headphones into his ears. Ben rolls his eyes – and *is that eyeliner?* Cara wonders, though what does it matter? What does she care? He laughs, shaking his head. Then Helen's sniggers reach her too.

Cara's twins still glow, despite the afternoon's flat glare, despite Ben's contrived darkness, and: *How close they'll always be*, she thinks. How interwoven. That bond between them, which has frequently held Cara distant, that at times keeps *everyone* at bay, it remains tangible. Unbreakable.

And Cara considers, as she so often has, what it must be like to have that? To have another person so rigorously, truthfully, a part of you? To have someone *forever*, and not just walking beside you, but inside you too? A connection that's sunk deep into your bones, that wavers with the thinner air between you.

They share such a careful, ice-blue gaze –

Suddenly it strikes Cara, that carefulness. The fact that while neither child has seemed to pay even a second of attention to their ancient goddess, they haven't walked over her, or even anywhere close to her – and Cara finds herself ridiculously pleased. Their avoidance is gratifying. An acknowledgement, surely, in itself.

My children, she thinks.

69

My magical, mysterious twins, *so precious*.

Of course she would never once have considered leaving them. She's never even allowed them to have to look for her, to wait for her. She *couldn't* have lost them. It's an impossible concept. Not even out here, in these woods –

And Tammy?

Tammy rummages about the clearing, circling Cara and her twins. Skidding about in that world of her own, mud spattering her wellies already – another smudge on her chin. What *has* she been doing?

But Cara's vision is smearing. The holly's different greens blur, while the bare branches merge into that blank, torn sky. It is only when Tammy marches, almost decisively, back to the woman, that everything refocuses.

The child pauses, open-mouthed, over that featureless face. For a heartbeat, she holds herself still, and then she bends, slowly. She doesn't wobble in her usual Tammy way.

Finally, she crouches.

Cara hardly breathes.

She cannot move. Her beloved boots are frozen to the frozen ground – and yet at the same time, a fine, fluttering part of her is sinking alongside Tammy.

Feeling him roll her over, feeling his mouth on her neck.

The give of that earth beneath her knees –

But Cara doesn't have to battle to bring herself back this time. Back to her third child, to her youngest, because Tammy is reaching out with one mittened fist.

70

She plants a single feather, and her tepid hair's spilling
as she looks back up, as she calls over.

   "Hey, Mummy, don't be sad."

The Insect Room

I still dream of 'The Insect Room', of visiting the museum with my father. It isn't far away, despite the years. Sometimes it's right there, waiting, when I close my eyes. A secret place inside me.

Outside, it was always raining – at least, that's how it seems when I look back. I remember a pewter rain-light at the window and a constant, muffled tapping. Wet footsteps squeaking on the parquet floor, a damp smell drifting from the walls... Knowing that it was time, I would slip away from my father. I'd wander 'The Insect Room' alone.

I didn't go far though. "Stay in sight," he'd tell me, although in all those grey and gleaming Sundays, I don't think I ever caught him gazing back at me. Not once.

But, glancing over my shoulder or from the corners of my eyes, it was always strange to see him there. A giant, surrounded by cabinets and cases of thin clean glass, by row upon row of tiny bodies. A still quite young man, a fit and handsome man, frozen in that dripping, old man's place. It was strange, really, to think of him at all.

He wasn't supposed to be walled in, in quiet rooms. It didn't suit him. He looked most at home in a pub garden in the summer, wielding a pint and a broad, yellowish smile, surrounded by friends, or family, by kids like me. Leaning forward with his punch-lines, his sleeves rolled up – his forearms brown and strong and oddly dusty in the golden August light. Brushing the flies away with careless fingers. Unthinking, himself.

75

But there, in 'The Insect Room', my father was someone else entirely. His face was serious and his movements awkward as if he had forgotten how to manage his height and bulk. One moment, he appeared to me thug-like – the next, some deep, daydreaming type. His coat didn't help. As he moved heavily between the cabinets and their shadows, that long tan trench coat made him look like an undercover detective, or perhaps a mobster, from an afternoon film. Whatever he was, I didn't know him there. During those regular visits, he wasn't mine.

But I would tell myself not to worry, not to panic. I knew that afterwards, things would be all right again. I'd claim him back.

Afterwards, in the car, he always gave me chocolate. Smarties or buttons, or my favourite, a bar of simple Dairy Milk, those snapping chunks cold from the glove compartment, but quickly warming, melting, in my eager hands. Several minutes had to pass before he turned the key in the ignition and we drove slowly away, readying ourselves in stages to face the house.

But he would come back to me during those moments while I ate chocolate and he fiddled with the radio. He'd rediscover his bad jokes along with the right station through the static; he'd find his deep singing voice too and his questions about school. His usual colour would chase the chalk from his stubbled cheeks and the rain on the car window would glitter sharply, a dazzle of beads and tight, bright strings. And through the rain, beyond the carpark, there would be a gentle seaweed ripple, the distant sigh of swaying trees.

But studying him in 'The Insect Room' as he stooped forward, perhaps squinting and leaving his clumsy breath like a cobweb smeared across the glass, he was that stranger. And I'd turn away, swinging around to view the nearest exhibit, or else I'd walk off briskly, striding with grim determination deeper into the cloying quiet. I would immerse myself in this Aladdin's cave, where the treasures were all neatly pinned and labelled, and long dead.

It wasn't just 'The Insect Room' – the entire museum was unnerving. It wasn't like the wide, white and airy places they had in town with constantly evolving Themes and interactive features, and people called 'Explainers' dressed in green. This museum was simply a random display of stray things and found things, of hunted things mainly. To reach our room, tucked away in its clay-smelling corner of the damp first floor, we had to walk through a menagerie of stuffed animals. There were the predictable moth-eaten deer and foxes and hares, and a single crouching lioness, with disconcerting amber eyes. Countless birds lined the staircase, many of them suspended, caught forever mid-flight.

We scarcely glanced at them. It was always 'The Insect Room' we headed for, without exception. The exhibits there never changed, and as I ambled past the filigree paper pockets of an abandoned wasp's nest, or a winding giant centipede, or a beetle so gold it was surely fake, I thought the same thoughts every time. Who were the people who put this place together, who wrote out all those labels in that cramped, calligraphic hand? And how did they manage the preservation? Surely you couldn't honestly stuff a bee...

With my father left somewhere behind me, when I reached the butterfly tables I always stopped.

Although they were undoubtedly the most beautiful part of 'The Insect Room', the butterflies were kept diligently covered. A grey weighted cloth hung over each glassed board to protect them from the light, or maybe from visitors who weren't quite curious enough. I would peel the cloths back carefully, breathlessly. I'd take a moment to step back, before I stared.

There were so many of them, perhaps thirty pinned to every board – there must have been two hundred altogether. And they were all so sad and delicate and pretty. Unique and precious, like separate secrets. Even their names were steeped in colour and magic; sometimes I'd murmur them aloud.

"Brimstone, Orange Tip, Grizzled Skipper, Meadow Brown."

Each one of them was amazing, both vivid and unreal, like the dazzling scraps that return sometimes from half-remembered dreams. But I had my favourites and I always saved the very best butterfly, mounted on the middle board, until last.

"Blue Morpho."

Impossibly huge and impossibly frail and all the way from Costa Rica, its silken wings were such a true clear blue that it made my eyes swim. My heart –

There was no point in trying to resist it. I would think about my mother.

I never wanted to dwell on her, as I didn't want my father to think about her either, but despite the distance I'd put between us, I would imagine my Dad's worries scurrying over the cabinets towards me. Earwig thoughts, they'd burrow gently, but persistently, into the sides of my head. Even at the museum, there was no escaping them – perhaps especially, at the museum – because it contained the memory of my mother's dress too. It was right there, in front of me, that Costa Rican blue.

I only ever saw that dress once, but it never left me. It was long and sequinned, perfect in the way that a tropical lagoon might be said to be perfect. The fabric poured from her fingers, a shimmer of jewelled dragonflies hovering above... There was something so complete about that dress that it almost hurt.

I watched her try it on. Slowly, cautiously – she held it up before her naked body in the same wondering way in which I always raised the covers from the butterfly boards. And she continued to take her time, slithering it on.

The bedroom mirror wasn't quite long enough and hung awkwardly, and so she had to climb up on to the mattress to see herself full length. I watched her soft pink heels catching in the sheets and then, through the mirror, I saw her eyes grow huge.

I understood that there was mystery in that dress, as well as beauty – I recognised it from the way in which she took it from her wardrobe, not from a hanger, but from the wide, slim box where it was folded, kept on the hard-to-reach top shelf. From the way that she fetched it only after Dad had gone out, when she thought she was alone. She never knew that I was there that last day, watching.

But my memory of that dress was so vibrant, so tangible, that sometimes I doubted its reality. Perhaps I'd made it up from wanting, from butterfly wings and shadows and the press of silvery light? Perhaps I had simply dreamt it – in the sharp, clean way that I dream of my childhood still.

Except there had been other mysteries towards the end. There was that same song that she used to play over and over, and the phone calls that would come for her too late at night... Long after her side of the bed had emptied, there were times when I thought I heard her, still. Her hushed voice fluttering among the house's other small dark breezes.

No wonder 'The Insect Room' didn't help. Nothing helped – not the bees or the roaches or the locusts or the spiders. And especially not the butterflies...

You could see it from the weight in my father's head, and from the way he moved his hands, pinching the bridge of his nose and rubbing his mouth. His cottony breath streaking the glass. Finally, I'd draw the cloths back down over the butterflies and walk across to him, hoping that he was ready. A cool marble trapped inside my throat as I anticipated the moment in the car when he'd come back to me.

He always came back to me, I had that, at least – and I had chocolate while I waited. Rain, like wing-beats, on the roof.

Maybe in America

Soon after take-off, Lucy woke. She tasted something sweet but grimy, old pennies on her tongue, and briefly, she imagined a way through. While the sensation didn't last, it was the first time since Maisie's accident that she had felt anything approaching hope and *maybe,* she caught herself thinking.

Maybe in America...

The storm enveloped the cabin soon after they'd ascended. Nobody expected it. Back on the ground, the day had fluttered with sunshine, planes transforming into shiny-new Dinky toys each time they hit the blue.

And the tremors were soft to begin with. The passengers went on fumbling with their magazines and headphones. At first, only the children paid attention. The children and the babies.

Listening, Lucy held herself as carefully as glass.

"Mummy? What's happening? Mu-um-meee... *How long till we're..."*

The toddler's whining tangled with an infant's wails and although Lucy suspected that Alex was also listening, she didn't look over, as he didn't look at her. As their elbows lay side-by-side, but did not touch.

Then the clouds took hold and the plane began to shake with a violence that nobody could ignore. Lucy's window turned milky, glazing over before it darkened. She wanted to close the blind, but wasn't allowed and so she refocused on the turbulence – the jolts in her ankles, the warble of the pilot's voice.

"A little weather," he said, fooling no one.

The plane rocked and the engines' roar grew. Their rushing muffled the baggage bumping overhead, but did nothing to drown out the children's cries.

That must have been when Alex reached for her hand – and it was only then that Lucy started to wonder about how serious things were; she pictured the plane dropping like something from a B-movie. A steaming crater in the ground.

Alex's thumb pressed more urgently into her palm and Lucy stared at their linked fingers. She tasted metal, but just before that revelation, that *maybe*, another quicksilver possibility flashed through her.

A different way out –

But too soon, the storm was over. The pilot chuckled, mocking his own relief. The babies settled. Alex's grip fell away, but for several seconds, Lucy's hand remained curled mid-air. Her fingers only then remembering how to hold on.

"Maybe, in America," Alex's mother had whispered, at the terminal. "Maybe, you'll work things out..."

Peggy had leant deep into Alex's shoulder, crumpling his shirt. As if it was thirty years ago and this, his first day at school; she couldn't seem to let her boy go.

After providing a lift to the airport, she'd remained with them until check-in, pretending to help. Her need to be involved was understandable. After all, Peggy was supposed to have minded Maisie during this holiday. Back in their other life, when they'd booked this silly second honeymoon, it had been intended as a treat for Grandma as much as a break for Lucy. And while Lucy had only just recalled this fact, Peggy would never have forgotten.

But as they parted, there was no malice in the older woman's face. There was barely anything; her creased skin was as pale as cotton. Without wanting to, Lucy remembered the sheet falling in slow-motion, its careful, snowdrift folds.

But nobody mentioned Maisie. No one wondered, at least aloud, if it might not be too soon? *Only nine months since...* As they'd never once voiced the irony of taking a 'road trip' either.

When Alex had reminded her of the holiday, just weeks earlier, Lucy had agreed because it was easier to nod than talk. But on reaching San Francisco, she believed she'd made a mistake after all. Yet another mistake in her great, stacked pyre. It *was* too soon. It was wrong. Even going through the motions was hard work.

The tourist maps and guide books. The hotel breakfast, where the other guests appeared large and loud, where everything seemed overly big and bright – the gleaming cutlery and glossy pastries, the bowls swollen with watermelon, luridly pink. Lucy scattered crumbs and seeds across her plate. She could hardly swallow.

On their first day, they walked the Bridge. According to Alex, it was the thing to do. The Bridge was crowded. Cars and trucks rattled past, battering the already wind-whipped air. Lucy tried to form the correct responses, wondering how an ordinary tourist might react to those H-shaped girders, to the traffic's oily stink. But her dogged attempts at staying *there*, in the moment, soon fell flat. At best, she felt like a bad actress – and while she told herself that even that was

85

OK, apt for California – it wasn't enough. Beyond the orange cables, the sea greyed.

"Intense dislocation," the therapist had said.

It was one of his favourite expressions, that, alongside 'traumatised' – but Lucy could never take in that word's true meaning. Instead she'd think 'Appletise', 'Tizer', recalling the fizz she'd guzzled as a child – drinks she'd never have allowed Maisie to even try, because of the sugar...

Alex marched ahead, click-click-clicking with his camera, dutifully capturing the crashing froth below and the groundbreaking engineering. The signs offering potential suicides advice: "There is Hope. Make that Call."

And naturally Lucy wondered if, in freefall, she might escape, but she couldn't have cracked during the crossing, not on that bridge, suspended. When she considered the scouring waves, all she thought, senselessly, was *trauma-tides*. It wasn't until two days later, at Golden Gate Park, that she crumpled.

They ended up in the Japanese Tea Garden, which surely ought to have been a shallow place with its entry fee and water features, its Buddhas and wind chimes. Yet somehow it managed to retain some elegance, perhaps even a genuine peace.

That was probably why Alex thought that Lucy finally broke down there, turning towards him as the day misted. Abruptly blinded by tears, she found herself burrowing helplessly, as mole-like as his mother...

She never told Alex about the fortune cookie. Her message, which had read: "You're lucky! You'll live a long and fruitful life."

It was Lucy's fault that Maisie had died. This was the knowledge that she was supposed to exist with, that Alex also had to struggle with, every day. Every dragging hour.

Sometimes she wondered how different things would have been if it hadn't been her, but Alex who had been at home that morning...

But such scenarios were ultimately as unimaginable as the facts were indisputable. Alex was working all day, *that day*, and Lucy was the one meant to be looking after Maisie – not standing in the kitchen trying to breathe, longing for five minutes, *just five minutes*, to herself.

It was Lucy who didn't watch as Maisie tottered through the conservatory doors, and then on towards the unlatched gate. Out, to the road beyond.

It was Lucy alone who heard the screech of brakes and felt the thud –

Of course it was Lucy. Only Lucy.

As it had been Lucy who'd always struggled with parenthood, a part of her shutting down right from the start.

Lucy assumed that her teary release amid the Bonsai was a random blip, but to her surprise, the loosening was just beginning. For the first time since Maisie, she was able to taste her own tears and once they took to the road, she went on feeling an unfolding, some quiet, internal shift.

And maybe...

Because Alex continued to look at her, meeting her eye in the rear-view mirror as he drove. He touched her too, gentle fingers on her wrist or knee. Lucy didn't deserve such comforts, and yet she found herself accepting them. Even as she suspected that, again, she'd have to pay.

But in Yosemite, the kindness only grew. It was in the air, netted between the turquoise birds and spinning pollen. There was a mercy to this landscape as overpowering as its beauty.

Whereas Lucy had been a clumsy giantess in the Tea Garden, here that universe was reversed. Everything towered, the biblical cliffs and silken sky, the green water and blue meadows, downy with wildflowers. The rusty Sequoias were among the earth's tallest trees, their charred trunks wide enough to drive a truck through, their pinecones as big as babies' heads...

Overwhelmed, Lucy discovered that a small part of her – a long buried part – simply loved this place; she loved this shrinking. And she'd thought that she would never love anything again.

And every night in Yosemite, she wept. She touched her tears in wonder, while even at midnight the pine scent crept into their room, slipping between the mosquito screens, outfoxing the air-con. The evergreen added its own sweet damp to the perspiration on Alex's hands as he reached across the shadows. It was the first time that they'd held each other, since Maisie.

Afterwards, sliding towards sleep, Lucy felt the black velvet forest pressing closer and other memories returned. They came carefully. Glimpses of happiness – how Maisie had looked, curled in her pyjamas – her gingerbread smell. *There had been happiness.*

As Lucy began to let herself remember, she felt the waterfalls dropping through the darkness. The great trees sighing.

But after five bright days and five secret, precious nights, it was time to move on. Lucy spent most of the nine hours to Vegas dozing, or pretending to. She kept her eyes determinedly closed while the temperature rose with increasing drama as the road wound down towards Death Valley. When Alex pulled over to take more photos, she merely peeked at the scorched landscape through hot, red lashes, and willed him back to the car.

Vegas was a predictable relief. Driving in, wedged between countless other honking, shimmering vehicles, Lucy gawped. Beneath the MGM gold lion and an equally monster-sized Coke bottle, crowds thronged the strip. A fishnet leg draped twenty storeys. But Lucy smiled at the exploding fountains, and at the plastic versions of far worthier cities – hotel-casinos called Venice and Paris. 'New York, New York', a roller-coaster threading its fake spires.

Everything was absurd, but Lucy liked it. After all, she couldn't remember the last time she'd felt anywhere near ridiculous. And Alex was grinning; as soon as they reached their hotel, they headed for the bar.

They shared a jug of potent cocktail, seated in a booth between an aquarium and a bank of one-armed bandits. While the world outside heaved and sweltered, the gambling spaces were cool and wide. Cave-like, except without the mystery, or quiet.

Noise layered noise. There were bells and hooters, laughter, groans. Electronic chimes feigned slithering money and three different chart tunes played at once.

A tangible madness glistened through the ringing and singing. Perhaps it was infectious?

After they'd finished their pitcher, it was Alex who called the sequinned waitress for another. As it was Alex who suggested that, just for fun, they played roulette.

Lucy was weaving on her feet by then, unable to tell where her dizziness ended and the general giddiness began. She hadn't let herself drink in months. She hadn't dared. But then, she wasn't really herself anymore. Not in America.

It'll be ok, she thought; she'd merge with the frivolity, give herself up to the emptiness. *Going, going, gone...*

Except that suddenly she wasn't sure how long she'd been sitting beside that particular roulette wheel. Across the table, a red-faced man with a gold tooth blew her a smoke-ring and she giggled, wanting to tell Alex, but Alex was gambling. He looked flushed, his sleeves rolled up, but he was half-smiling, half-frowning as he did when listening to a new CD or admiring a painting and Lucy hadn't seen that expression in almost a year. With a flurry of excitement, she followed his familiar beautiful hands, smoothing chips across the baize.

She watched the wheel spin. Red and black and white swept by, the croupier's fingers dancing like a magician's. Lucy reeled, but the little, clicking ball found its place and then there was a fresh pile of chips in front of Alex.

We're winning, Lucy realised.

Laughing, she caught her husband's eye. He smiled right back and again, they were connected, this

90

new woozy Lucy and this winning Alex. We've made it, she thought, all the way to Vegas.

Tonight, there would be no darkness between them, nothing to separate them. No Maisie –

Except that then the colour faded from Alex's face. He paled just as he had on the plane, only he was looking directly at Lucy now; she could see herself inside his eyes – she could see herself more clearly than she ever had before.

She saw how the laughter clung to her even as her make-up blurred. She saw how she glittered – a tipsy woman, a carefree woman. A woman who'd left the garden gate open, who had wanted five minutes, *just five minutes*, to herself.

93

My Secret Sister

I have two sisters. There's my real sister and then there is my secret sister. My real sister, being four years and two days older than me, has of course been around forever. I can't remember how long my secret sister's been here. She could have turned up just a couple of months ago; she might have been born with the heat-wave... Now and then, she does look newborn.

At noon, when the days are bright enough to make us blink, her skin appears raw and rubbery, purple-tinged like a baby mouse's, or a cuckoo chick's, before the fur or feathers have grown in. But there's that granny-thing about her too, years scribbled into the cracks around her eyes.

My secret sister was definitely there that night when they left me alone in the house. She was waiting in my bed after my real sister had climbed, long-legged, into the ambulance beside Mum – but maybe that wasn't the first time that she came? It's difficult to remember anything properly, this summer's been going on so long.

And every evening now, after lights-out, she's here.

It's way too hot for the duvet, but I pull it over my head anyway; I bury myself and after a while, my secret sister crawls in beside me. She fills the duvet's cottony gaps, all its seedy pockets. She fills the spaces around my hips and elbows too. And once we're locked together, tight as puzzle pieces, she strokes her wiry fingers through my hair. Cat-like, she laps my face for tears. She pinches –

My secret sister is nothing like my real sister.

My real sister has spots and a bottle of Clearasil. She has heated curling tongs and a padded bra as curved and rigid as a pair of ice-cream scoops that my secret sister and I like to play with.

I put the bra on my head and pretend that I have ears-on-top like Mickey Mouse.

"Hey, Goofy! Goofy – hey!" I squeak, or something like that – until my secret sister snatches it from me.

She also lifts the bra, but she doesn't strap it on over her knotted hair like I do. What she does is blind herself, covering her eyes as if the bra is an enormous pair of swimming goggles. My secret sister never looks anything like a swimmer though; she looks more like a fly – a giant, blind fly. I don't like it.

"Buzz, buzz," she sings anyway. "Buzz, buzz, buzz."

"Have you been in your sister's things again?" Mum asked when I visited the hospital.

She said it slowly, her voice broken and crackly because of the great bowls of air – bowls bigger than bra-cups or ice-cream scoops – that she has to drink in between each word. She couldn't get out of bed that day to shake me.

She lay at the other end of her private room, propped up against the pillows in the patchy dim. The curtains were drawn against the sweating streets outside, but another whole strange city sprawled between us, made up of her hulking armchair, stacked with linen, and the domes of her oxygen tanks. Beyond those shadowy shapes, Mum seemed far away, she couldn't reach me; nevertheless, I felt shaken.

"You girls," she said. "Can't you just leave each other be?"

Mum has more than enough to deal with without us fighting; she shouldn't need to tell us that –

But, *secretly,* we've had enough too, my real sister, my secret sister and I. Not that we'd say anything either. When Mum gets cross her breathing gets worse.

"I'll bang your heads together," she says. And once, she actually did it.

She *did* – when I close my eyes, I can still feel the ringing. Except Mum claims that never actually happened, so maybe it didn't after all.

Both my real sister and my secret sister like to pinch. They both leave bruises, although they're very different in shape and colour. My real sister's are ordinary blurry things that change from red to mauve to yellowish-green, whereas my secret sister's marks are always the faded blue of old tattoos. They're also tattoo-shaped. There have been birds, maybe swallows, and a broken heart. Once there was something that might have been a fat mermaid if it wasn't a koi carp.

My sisters have always given me their different bruises for different reasons. My real sister pinches because I have spilt her eye-shadow or messed up the alphabetical order of her CD collection or left a bowl of Branflakes to harden like cement beside our beds. Some days, she punches or kicks instead of pinching. Some days, she pulls my hair.

Up until recently, my secret sister has only ever pinched, and she has never done it because I'm

97

irritating. *It's because I love you*, she whispers. *It is because you are all mine.*

My secret sister has a naughty streak. She likes to lock us in and hide the keys so that my real sister can never leave the house on time; when neighbours drop by, we have to speak through the door. And when I used to wash up, she'd smear food onto the plates I'd already stacked into the drying-rack – but what my secret sister enjoys the most is stealing things from shops.

Whenever Mum, wanting softer tissues or fresh deodorant, sends me down to the pharmacy on the hospital's ground floor, my secret sister pockets the blackcurrant-flavoured cough sweets – and sometimes, I suspect, she has swiped Mum's money too.

As I search Mum's huge handbag for change (removing the furry hairbrush and forgotten lipsticks, the battered library romance that is always overdue) I've caught my secret sister hopping along the tampon aisle and *jingling*, her gaze ice-bright with giggling.

"Giggle-pots," Mum used to call us, back when my real sister still looked at me.

Apart from the hospital, my real sister doesn't go anywhere with me anymore. Throughout this stretching summer of ambulances and visiting hours and bruises shaped like birds, only my secret sister still comes to the heath.

Traipsing a path between the sagging nettles, she skips around me, sometimes shrinking into the corners of my eyes, sometimes leaping forward or backwards, to grab at me. She catches my hand then; she *squeezes*, before yanking me on. Despite the sticky heat, my secret sister likes the heath; she's especially impressed with the grave there.

It isn't really a grave of course – that's just what my real sister used to say; it's only a mound of earth covered with the same dry grass as everything else, except that somehow, it's separate.

My sisters and I believe – or at least some of us used to believe – that there's a sheep buried under there. A Sacrificial Lamb. It's probably because of all those hymns we used to sing, about Jesus being an actual lamb – although there's something creepy about a sheep's golden eyes, the way that their pupils slit right through.

Still, we go on sitting beside our mound, my secret sister and I. And as if we're back between those draughty pews, we pray.

Dear Dead Sheep,

Please may the dentist get cancelled on Thursday.

Please may I have some new jeans, only not from the catalogue.

Please may it be baked beans on the side, always, and never peas.

Please may Mum's treatment work this time –

The dead sheep, I think, is a bit like Father Christmas. He never gives you quite what you hoped for, but you have to keep on believing, just in case.

Last week, at the heath, my secret sister refused to stick to the mound's edges. She slithered through the bleached blades and burnt-looking dirt, and then lay, splayed like a starfish, across the grave.

Her hair spread out in ripples, merging with the yellow grass. I blinked even harder than usual – she *glowed*. My own hair is lank, rank, where it hasn't been washed, and I'd always thought that my secret sister's hair was also dark – but then the sun slipped behind a rare cloud and it was again.

I lay down flat on top of her. Up close, the grave smelt like old wrinkled apples. Even empty, Mum's room still smells that way sometimes, but I didn't move, not for a while; I just practised my breathing – until the horrible thoughts started coming.

What if my real sister was under there, only not as she was now, but how she'd been before, when we used to play together? What if I'd somehow accidentally left her there, my real, old sister –

And then: What if this was Mum's grave?

What if Mum's already dead, completely dead, lying dead under there, right now?

I wanted to jump up. I wanted to run, but my secret sister wrapped me tight in her spiky arms. She would not let me go.

Since Mum was taken back into hospital the last time, my real sister thinks that she's the boss of the whole world. She makes me fold the laundry after she has brought it in from the line and hisses "*shut up, shut up,*" to me whenever she's on the phone – which is a lot. She also sends me out for supplies with never enough money. My secret sister and I believe that she does this on purpose because of the things that we steal instead. Because of the pre-packed BLT sandwiches and the sushi and the cough sweets.

At least my real sister has stopped making me wash up. Over the summer, used plates and pans have built up steadily around the kitchen, forming another new weird city. They've crept from the counter tops up on to the bread bin and across the freezer roof, where they're regularly visited by touring parties of flies. Slow, dizzying creatures with fat and glinting bodies.

"Buzz, buzz," I sing along with them as they sink and crawl and circle. "Buzz, buzz, buzz..."

Up in our bedroom, I'm sure that my secret sister will pinch me – but then it comes to me that I haven't been pinched for days, maybe weeks; the bruises are fading. And I wonder if my secret sister is annoyed?

When Mum was last home, a while ago now, I decided to show her my bruises. I undressed and left the bathroom door unlocked and waited, chilled. Eventually, Mum blundered in, just as I'd planned. She gasped – but then, doesn't she always?

"Excuse me," she said as she retreated, but that was all. A quick, sharp click as she shut the door.

But my secret sister, I realise, isn't angry; she just has a different plan.

Instead of pinching, she hands me the Stanley knife. She tells me that it will work better than the bruises, better than pinching, and far, far better than praying to an invisible dead sheep.

And afterwards, she'll clean the red from my skin, exactly as she wipes the tears and heath-seeds from my sleep-soft body. And I think about how gentle she is, mostly. I think about her rough-soft kitten tongue –

And although my real sister is suddenly standing there in the doorway – standing *right there, right now*, boggle-eyed and gawping – my secret sister keeps on murmuring, reassuring me. Explaining how even this is ok, because of course my real sister can't truly see me – just like Mum didn't see me –

Like no one properly exists in the hospital's half-light...

But if I do this, with the knife – if I do it just this once, and do it right, like my secret sister says – then maybe the flies might clear off, maybe the heat will break? Maybe Mum will come back home.

Fever

It was three in the morning when he thought he heard his daughter screaming. Not crying or calling, just screaming. There were no words in that sound, no caught breath – a raw outpouring that made the darkness quiver as he fumbled back the duvet and half-leapt, half-staggered towards the hole of thicker shadow that he hoped was still the hall.

There was no more time for lights than there was for proper thinking. With that noise, his head flooded with unformed snatches – *an attacker – a man in the house – a dark, dark woman.*

Ellen, he thought.

And then: *Baby, oh, my baby-girl – Katy, I'm coming. I'm nearly...*

Panic thumped and battered, trapped moths under his skin. The hallway walls rippled and bristled like great furred flanks. Between their scratchy blackness, he almost fell.

Before the noise, he'd been sleeping deeply, dreaming of the girl's mother again, *of Ellen.* Briefly, he pictured her, rising haltingly from her knees, one hand covering her eye –

The screaming continued to spiral, the sound sharpening further as, at last, he reached Katy's door.

If it had been daytime, he would have been able to see her home-made name-plate with its glitter and stickers. This room so obviously belonged to a child, a little girl – *shit!* – even by torchlight, it would be clear.

And what are they doing to her? My only –

He thought his sweating fingers would miss the handle, but it turned smoothly, the door gliding open. Now he slapped at the wall for the light-switch – then winced and swayed, struggling to see through the sudden glare. The dazzle was blotted by gaps, holes that might have been pulsing planets, black suns. He had to blink to see through them, to find his daughter –

She was sitting up in bed, her eyes unblinking.

And with the light stunning the night into submission, he understood belatedly that the screaming had also stopped – although the room somehow contained it still. Between Katy's purple furniture and staring bears, the air felt shredded.

But: "Daddy," she said, and her voice was soft. "I want my Daddy."

As he moved towards her, the air condensed. He smelt the sour fug of recent sleep and her cherry-flavoured medicine. The bears stared down at him from the toy hammock, but there was no one there, no attacker.

There was only his girl, Katy, sitting up in her great mound of duvet, her ginger hair a tangled nest, her small face flushed. Her eyes black, and looking beyond him.

"Nightmare?" he said.

He resisted the urge to cross the room to the window. He knew that it was closed – he'd locked it himself during the afternoon – and there wasn't space for anyone to hide behind the curtains. Nor would there be someone outside, standing in the pooled shadows between the streetlamps, looking up. He didn't need to check there – or under the bed either, which contained only the usual collection of lidless pens and absurdly tiny Barbie shoes.

"Daddy?" Katy said.

He stepped awkwardly between her stunted furniture and then sank to a crouch, his knees cracking. He clutched at her bedside cabinet to steady himself, and then recoiled at the stickiness. He glanced from his pink-gummed palm to the puddle of spilt medicine and remembered her fever – he could hardly believe he'd forgotten it. He thought he understood the screaming.

"It's ok, Katy," he said. "I'm here."

He'd had terrible fevers, himself. The usual round of childhood illnesses had sent his temperature soaring, his head spinning, and he had often seen things that weren't there. Actually, it was just the one thing, the same thing, again and again...

He reached out to his daughter, his hand casting a paw-like shadow over her duvet. She flinched before he could touch her, so that he caught the heat lifting from her in greasy waves, but not the flushed skin underneath it.

"I want my Daddy," she whispered. "I want to go home," and he understood how frightened she was. His heart banged faster.

"You are home," he told her. "You're safe. You're here. And I'm right here too..."

She went on staring, not quite at him, but through him, her black gaze concentrated somewhere between his cheekbone and his chin.

"I don't want you," she said. "I want my Daddy."

He shuddered, unable to stop himself. His slamming heart froze. What was she staring at?

In a rush, his fever memories returned – cracks opening in the flocked wallpaper of his childhood home, a gap widening to reveal a tunnel. It had been impossible to turn away as the gap became clearer,

107

transforming into a street, a dirty alleyway. He remembered it clearly – the alley's over-spilling rubbish bins, the brown walls glistening as though with sweat.

He'd known it couldn't be real. There had only been square lawns and trimmed hedges beyond the neat bricks of his suburban house. The alleyway hadn't existed – at least, not there.

And yet there it was, every time a fever had overtaken him; he'd see those bins caught in the grimy light, the cracked paving stones and the damp gutter clotted with something like hair. And between those bins, there would be the shadows that he knew weren't just shadows – at any moment, they might rise...

He thought of his dream, of Ellen rising, and a queasy warmth spread through him – had he caught his daughter's virus? He made himself breathe evenly. Katy needed him. He was her father, who loved her. He knew who he was –

But still, his little girl shrank from him. She looked more fragile than ever, with a dense noose of shadow separating her fine boned neck from her fleecy pyjama collar, her twig-like wrists swamped by her cuffs. The most solid thing about her was her heat. Beneath the medicine's bright tang and the fustiness of sleep, that heat was flavoured by a familiar sickroom scent, yeasty and rotten, like greening bread...

From his daughter's bunched shoulders, he knew that she didn't want him to touch her, not yet, and there was a sneaking relief in that. Generally, they weren't overly tactile. Sometimes, at nursery, Katy seemed almost painfully self-sufficient; she'd never had much trouble managing her buttons and buckles; she could already tie her laces. The nursery workers smiled appreciatively when he picked her up. They knew he was a single parent; "It's tough," they told him, gently, repeatedly. "You're doing a grand job." And while he suspected that if he'd been a woman they might have been less charitable, he always shrugged humbly in response. His air of quiet, he knew, was to his advantage.

He kept his voice low now: "It's ok, Baby. You're just sick. You'll be better soon. And I'm here; Daddy's here."

But her black gaze went on, and "Where?" she said. "Where's my Daddy?"

He heard the sigh whistle out of himself through gritted teeth. Her clock with the monkeys woven through each number told him that it was ten past three – and he couldn't give her any more medicine, not yet. He'd read the instructions with great care: *No more than six doses in twenty-four hours...* And he remembered what the doctor had said to his own mother all those years ago – how she mustn't panic about his crying, his hallucinations, how a fever was nothing to grow hysterical about; it was just a body's way of coping, of fighting.

But the way that Katy looked now, her hair caught in clumps and her cheeks flaming... It wasn't only that her appearance was such a contrast to the clean, smiling child he fetched every day from nursery, it was as if, somehow, she might no longer be her true self either –

She looked like her mother, he realised.

The distinctive angles of Ellen's brow and jaw pressed insistently through Katy's features – she looked more like her mother than she had ever done before.

He rubbed his palm across his eyelids; he didn't want to think about Ellen. The way she'd looked, stumbling to her feet like something broken – like the ghost from that Japanese horror film – the one that he'd first watched, he remembered, on DVD, with her.

It had been back in his other life, *their* other life, back when they'd shared a tiny flat overlooking the tram station, where the electric flashes through the blinds had kept them company night after night. It had probably been three in the morning then too; in that early time, before Katy was born, they'd rarely wanted sleep. There was too much talking to do, too much touching. They would drink together, or smoke, and there were times when the talking had stretched them to revealing hidden places, when they'd surprised themselves with their words, and with their bodies.

After the film, they'd been too scared to go to the toilet alone, although it was the first time that he'd pissed in front of a girl since he was five years old. Giggling, they'd sunk back on to the sofa, laughing even harder at first, as they discussed the movie. All those scenes of crawling, of that ghost-girl crawling, crawling out of the well, crawling right through the screen... Ellen had thought it was the idea that there weren't even any walls to break that made the film so very frightening. That you could simply climb straight through... Then he'd told her about the alley.

And in attempting to describe his fevers to Ellen in his stoned, wondering state, he'd played with the whole concept of worlds beyond worlds, taking it further. Wasn't love another version of that? Weren't there times when it seemed to reveal other sides, not just a sharing of your true self with someone else, but a tangible sense of something *more*. That feeling of teetering on a brink, of peeling back secret layers and glimpsing...

But it wasn't just love that did that; when he'd been told that his mother had died, the first thing that he'd pictured was the alleyway.

And after Ellen –

Naturally, he didn't think about love that way anymore. *Hippy-shit* – it didn't help, not with the day-to-day, with the washing and the cooking and the bedtime stories, with the general getting on. What use was any such thinking tonight, with Katy running a temperature *and still glaring?*

"Would you like a glass of water?" he asked.

Katy didn't reply, not even to shake her head. Her gaze remained steady, unwavering, so set that it refused reflection. He couldn't find a hint of the room's light in her eyes. And when he leaned closer, nothing shifted. He might as well have been not there –

"Katy," he said, and he tried to keep the gruffness from his tone. "I'm talking to you. I asked you a question. Would you like some water? Answer me, Katy."

He watched her mouth move slowly; her bottom lip, hanging open, was ragged where she'd chewed it. Her whole face appeared sore. Her jaw tightened and in the seconds before she spoke, a renewed dread rolled through him. It was all too much, the screaming and his memories, and Katy, holding herself away from him, her little body, burning up. He didn't think he could stand it if he remained strange, a stranger, to her. His head ached. There was a balled tightness between his eyes. If she asked for her Daddy again, he feared that it might break, *shatter*, in a way that would offer no relief. He pictured flying shards, flesh giving and then splitting – and if she asked for her mother –

"Daddy," she said. "*My Daddy...* What's that in front of your face?"

He could have laughed then; he felt the laughter, like madness, bubbling inside him. With an enormous effort of will, he repressed it – as he resisted the sudden desperate urge to lift his own hands, to claw at his features. His cheeks were blazing; he thought they must be as livid as hers and he could almost feel a mask there, as sticky as cobwebs.

And he remembered how Ellen's expression had changed towards the end. There had been no love in her look, nothing that connected them, just a sneering disgust and worse, a kind of sympathy. Not that she'd looked at him much at all during those final months; since the birth, it seemed, she'd been hiding from him, disappearing, piece by piece...

Even on the last night, he'd felt as if she was deliberately erasing herself, half her face missing where in pain and shock she'd covered it. She had barely seemed real to him –

Except that she'd kept on rising. Rising despite him, and despite the blood flowering between her protective fingers –

Her blood, smeared across his knuckles too, and around the broken bottle clenched hotly in his fist – a fever raging –

Feeling half-blind himself now, he reached for his daughter. She cowered, but he couldn't hold back; *he loved her* – but as his arms closed around her, he gasped. What if his hands sank right through her? What if she vanished and he found himself beyond?

But there was just Katy, gathered against his chest. There was no way through, no other side.

112

He gazed down at her bowed head, at her knotted hair, at her tiny shoulder-blades pressing like budded wings through her pyjamas. She shivered and he pulled her closer. He began to rock. He shut his eyes, trying to concentrate only on holding her – but even her folded body brought back the alleyway. That final night –

And although Katy was so frail, so husk-like, he felt a horrible weight dragging at his shoulders –

Again, he saw that matted gutter, the brown perspiring bricks.

Again, those looming bins, their stink, and the spaces between them, the waiting gaps... And he remembered how as he'd attempted to set his burden down, the entire alleyway had flared into focus with the flash of a nearby tram – the terror had been overwhelming. What if the shadows rose? What if they refused to lie still?

He heard the screaming.

Once more, the screaming was everywhere.

He felt it tearing through his daughter's body, and through his own. It ripped him from her and bound her close.

He wrapped Katy tighter, unable to hear his own blurted sobs beneath the sounds. Her wet hot cheeks pressed against the curve of his jaw. He felt the silk of her lashes and wondered if she'd shut her black, black eyes at last, but again, he saw Ellen. He saw her stumbling nearer, as if daring him on. Her mouth slashing open –

He felt the pursed brush of Katy's lips.

He held his daughter from him. And as the screaming continued, shrill and barbed and never-ending, he saw that her eyes remained wide and dark, but that her mouth was closed.

Her mouth was closed, although the screams went on. And when her small lips finally parted, it was only to whisper.

"Daddy," she said. "Can you hear it too?"

On the Island

We were playing out, up on the ridge, when the alarm first sounded. It was the end of the day and the cold was coming in like flying glass. It caught in the matted fur around our hoods, swooped up our nostrils, glittered in our eyes.

"What's that?" said Lana, lifting her mitten to her mouth.

Her nose was crusted with dried snot and in the wind her hair stood up like stiff electric cables. She'd never wear a hat, not even when it hailed. She would have been just four.

"It's the alarm," I said, when nobody else would. "There's been a prisoner, escaped."

Lottie and Christopher wouldn't look at me. Lottie had a stick from somewhere. She whipped it back and forth, drawing patterns in the flattened grass, while Christopher crouched seriously over his bootlaces. But Lana's eyes grew wide and black. She was remembering the secret about me that she wasn't supposed to know.

Far below, beneath the ridge, the sea rocked and rose and burst, grey waves twisting and fighting like kittens in a box. The sun was disappearing in a hurry and the clouds were closing in. The changing light stuck to their bellies in bleeding threads.

The siren continued, on and on. It grew more insistent with every loop and when Lottie spoke, I saw her mouth move, but between the siren and the wind, her words were lost.

"We're to go home," Christopher said for her. "Dad said. When the alarm sounds, we're to go straight in."

We both stared at his boots. He'd only had them a week and they were as hard and shiny as polished conkers. He dragged them deliberately through the yellow mud.

"I don't want to go yet," Lana whined, but she was only saying it for saying it. She looked very small and blown and scared.

"Come on, Lana," I said and pounced on her. I caught her in my arms, her body spindly even through her padded coat. I started to run.

"Stop it, Joe. Put me down!"

But she was laughing as she shouted and *she knows me* I thought. *She knows who I really am. It will be all right.*

I refused to look back towards Christopher and Lana, to glimpse their panting faces.

We could run forever I thought as Lana gasped and squealed, warm against my banging chest. *We could just keep going.* Straight out over the ridge, and then beyond.

There's been a prisoner, escaped –

I couldn't think about it now.

I had to set Lana down when we reached the stile. The wooden posts were slimy, streaked black and green. I climbed over first, then waited, ready to grab her trembling arm when she realised, finally, that she couldn't do it on her own. A couple of sheep trundled over to watch us with their misted eyes. They had strands of shit clinging to their frothy tails, like chewing gum. Their breath hung before their faces, paler and more persistent than our own.

Lottie and Christopher were still a way behind us and I was glad. We were on their land now and we weren't supposed to run wild – we might scare the livestock. The clouds had sunk until they were almost on top of us, but the siren's sound pressed closer. When Lana smiled, I glanced away, determined not to cry.

They were my friends, the Petersons – Christopher, Lottie and little Lana. I had only been on the island for five months and already I'd made friends. Mum was so relieved.

"It's because they're not part of the local community," she'd explained, lighting another Benson. There were shadows around her eyes beneath the make-up, shadows within shadows. She was having trouble making friends here herself.

"They're outsiders, just like us," she said, but it wasn't true. There was no one quite like us.

The Petersons had moved here only a year ago, to start a small organic meat farm. Chickens and sheep and cows – though they'd already lost the cows by the time that Mum and I arrived. Nevertheless: "We're living out our dreams," Mrs Peterson had told me as she warmed me by her Aga on that first deadly-bitter night, and I'd nodded very slowly as if I knew exactly what she meant.

Hand in hand now, Lana and I galloped through the field. We leapt together over sprawling puddles and spiky nettle nests. The sheep didn't scatter as we approached, but stepped back quietly, as curt and disapproving as old ladies at a bus stop.

"Fuck," Christopher said, behind us. He'd caught something, a sleeve or trouser leg, on the wet splinters of the stile. He only swore because he'd turned fourteen two months ago. I heard Lottie, who was three years younger, start to giggle.

I was twelve at the time and Lana only four, but we ran together because Lana was the only one who really knew me. And she was fast for her age too, a natural, like a hunted, zigzagging hare.

The shudder of rotors joined the siren and the exhausted wailing of the wind, as a helicopter swung briefly into sight above the blackening trees. A light flared in our faces and disappeared, leaving us stunned and blinking. For a moment, like the first glare of snow.

The island had been covered in snow when Mum and I arrived. A meringue dropped thoughtlessly into the middle of the dirty sea. I'd thought it would melt immediately with all that salt about, but the island was tougher than it looked. That's probably why they built the prison here, why they sent Dad here after his fourth conviction.

"We've got to stay together, the three of us," Mum had said. She ripped the foil from her cigarettes, searched her pockets for the lighter.

Gran had wanted me to stay with her in the city, but Mum was having none of it. "Old cow," she said. "She doesn't understand. We're the only things keeping him together."

"Don't worry, Mum." I reached up to brush the blond strands out of her eyes. "It'll be all right."

But secretly, I'd begged Gran. More than anything, I had wanted to stay exactly where I was.

Now, the Petersons' farmhouse loomed ahead. Their windows twinkled like Christmas lights, though the thatch had been stripped away, replaced with gleaming tiles, like the roof of Lottie's glorious bubble-wrapped doll's house, abandoned half-unpacked, inside.

Lana slowed. *She doesn't want to leave me,* I thought, but "Listen," she said.

There was the sound of police cars, like in a Hollywood film – and I'd believed that there were only two of them for the whole island. I looked away from her excited grin. I was doing my absolute best, trying not to panic.

The red in the sky was already fading. Beside the farmhouse, I could just make out the skewed, chopped angles of the barns and outbuildings – I had explored them all with Lana, climbing the hay-bales and hanging from the doors of Mr Peterson's shiny new truck.

But it was the shed with the hooks and chains hanging from the ceiling that I thought of now, the one that smelt of dirt, of rot. I had only ever seen that building empty, but it had made me shudder anyway – I'd seemed to feel its waiting.

"I can't live without you," said Dad, the last time that we visited.

"This place," he murmured. "You don't understand. It's *killing* me."

Mum's fingertips trembled against his upon the table. I'd looked away, worried about what the guard might say if he spotted them. The pair of them huddled there, crying like babies.

121

"We love you," Mum said. "Whatever happens, whatever you decide, there's always us."

Outside, through the grille, the sun was a hard bright pebble in the sky, searing (I knew) at the edges of the snow, turning the perfect meringue coating of my crisp new world into pools of heartbreaking grey slush.

Lottie and Christopher caught up with us as we neared their back door. I saw Mrs Peterson between the slats of the blind. She was moving through the kitchen, her hair flashing the same silver as the polished pans hanging proudly from the beams.

Lana battered in to her through the open door and I thought how determinedly she'd lock up the house once all her children were inside. Out here, the siren tightened.

"Hey Mum!" I heard Lana call. "*Mum* – did you see the helicopter?"

She had forgotten me already.

"You can come in if you like," Christopher said, but he didn't mean it.

"Nah." I shrugged. "What for?"

"Oh, go on," Lottie whispered. She still had her branch, but she was leaning on it now as if it was a dancer's cane.

"Christopher!" Mrs Peterson called.

Lana had left the door wide open and the step was gleaming, a satisfying square of buttery light.

"We'd better go," said Christopher. His long fingers tugged at one other.

They're sorry for me, I realised. And then I felt like snatching Lottie's stick then and breaking it – *snap, snap* – in their gazing, sorrowful faces.

"Whatever," I said. "See ya."

122

I turned and ran.

Back across the black fields, out into the rising night, while the alarm went on reeling up around me.

I only glanced back once, but there was Lana at her bedroom window. She was jumping about and waving at me, probably poking out her tongue.

"I'll see you too, Lana," I whispered.

The ground skidded and sprayed beneath my feet.

"Whatever it takes," my father had promised from his separate side of the table and Mum had nodded, her teary eyes hardening, becoming tarnished metal.

By the time I reached our house, the police cars seemed to have vanished and even the helicopters had faded, ticking into the distance. I was hardly hearing the alarm anymore; it had been going on so long.

I turned my key in the lock and went inside. The junk cupboard in the hall was open and there were shoes and scarves and envelopes scattered across the peeling lino. I climbed over them on my way into the kitchen. The air looked hung with cobwebs from the cigarette smoke. Mum's shoulders jerked. She turned, her face stretched long and tired with waiting.

"It's you," she said, and remembered to smile.

The gaping fridge glowed blue. There was a tower of bread beside Mum's elbow. I watched her bracelets shiver as she smoothed a red-stained knife back and forth.

"What's that you're making?" I asked.

A canvas shopping bag bulged beneath the table. I saw some clothes inside and two of my books, a graphic novel and some babyish one I'd grown out of long ago – a man with an apple for a head on the front

123

cover. The bag could have been just jumble, except that Mum's pink beaded sandals lay across the top, one three-inch heel poking out, like a witch's bony finger. They were her very best shoes, the ones she used to wear when she and Dad would go out dancing.

"Just a few sandwiches –" Mum said and then the room imploded with a great bright nothingness. The prison alarm, we both realised, had come to a stop.

I saw myself inside Mum's eyes, a small wet shaking shape.

"Christ," she murmured and then there was a shot, and then silence, and then two more.

"*Mum,*" I said, but she wasn't looking at me now.

The jam jar went flying from her fist, the light sliding over it as it rolled gracefully mid-air. And before it landed, before the shatter, I pictured Lana at her window; I saw her jumping and waving, saying goodbye after all.

Second Person

5.33pm

You've reached your flat, your doorstep. At last, you stop, but you've scarcely any breath and your head goes on echoing with the harsh ticking of your heels. You still can't quite believe yourself, how you forgot your phone. Today, of all days. When you had promised you'd call as soon as you'd told him:

There's somebody else.

By two, you'd said.

By two o'clock, it was meant to be done. Your engagement over. The whole relationship, *everything*, over and done with –

No: your true life finally beginning –

Except that it's already

5.34pm

And you drop your keys, unless they're his keys – you made him give his set back. You bend awkwardly to retrieve them, unbalanced by your heavy bag. It slide-slumps from your shoulder to your elbow, the strap catching at your hair.

And then it's a battle to simply get past the door and even once you're in, you go on fighting yourself. Knocking your knee on the hall table so that later there will be a bruise, not unlike those others. The one on your neck, and those clouded purple petals circling your wrist. Not that any of that concerns you now –

The pathway to the kitchen, where your mobile surely waits, becomes a wind tunnel, sucking you on.

And it's there. *Thank god*, it's there.

It's on the counter beside the fruit bowl, which contains a single brown wrinkled apple, a skeleton of grape sticks. Your mobile, just lying there, like something innocent. In relief, you pounce. But in your hand –

5.37pm

The phone is lifeless.

You don't take your eyes from its screen as you rush through to the bedroom, to where the charger waits among a tangled nest of other wires. You squat clumsily to plug it in and your skirt rides up, revealing a milky slice of winter thigh. While you wait for the connection, you grow aware of the different places where your blouse is sticking. And that exposed skin goes on distracting you, the pale dimpled meat of it. Hastily, with your spare hand, you tug flat the crumpled cotton. You can't afford to think about your imperfections. About how, even after everything, with all you've given up and what you've finally confessed, you still might not be enough. With the first pulse of the battery bar, you dial.

5.40pm

Except apparently you can't. You couldn't. Not just yet. At least not without a glass of wine at your side. You've returned to the kitchen, where the light has deepened. With the sunset, the draining board's tinged red.

You ignore the red, just as you ignore the way your fingers tremble when you reach inside the cupboard. But you can't help wincing when the glasses knock together; their discordant chime reverberates right through you.

It's the fear.

The fear that despite all the planning and the longing, the fact that you've kept up your side of the bargain – that you've actually done it, *you've left him* – you might after all, remain alone.

You go to the fridge and as you pour, you're suddenly struck by a whole new guilt. A cold, far brighter and sharper than the slow pervasive mud-like sensation that you've been carrying for months. So clearly, you feel the waiting beyond yourself, and you know that this delay is madness.

In your renewed haste, clutching your Dutch courage, you leave the fridge open, purring, behind you.

5.55pm

But still, the phone goes on lying in the soft dark beside your bed.

You needed to finish the glass first. Although between each acrid sip, your afternoon kept returning in brittle sharp-edged pieces. How he slumped forward when you told him, the colours changing in his face. You'd never seen him cry like that before. Such a slow, sad breaking… It had been all wrong.

Of course it's wrong –

But you ought to sound happy when you call. You should raise your glass to your new future. You need to believe in that future, to trust it, to move beyond the fear. After all, you've done everything you were told to do. Except even now.

Even now.

There's too much love inside you. Too much hope.

What if...

129

You return to the kitchen to fetch the bottle. You go on pouring, drinking.

6.37pm

The bottle's empty.

Though you lost the last half-glass of it, tipping it stupidly, soaking your skirt. For a moment you simply sit, watching the stain. Feeling the wet, feeling caught out. You don't know how you'll explain this waiting, this delaying, why you still haven't called. *When you said – you promised – by two o'clock.*

What if this, in itself, is unforgivable?

In the next instant, you're up, fumbling with your waistband, desperate to be rid of the sodden fabric. As they're released, the skirt's poppers sound far louder than they should. *Snap, snap, snap –*

And there's your body again. Your legs. The pasty pinch-able flesh –

You cover up quickly. A pair of ancient pyjama bottoms, the first thing to hand. You can't stand your skin, that sallow gleaming, only made worse by the shadows. There are dirty grey flowers in every corner of your flat now – because it's grown so late. But the stink of your own sweat turns your stomach, and your breath's rough with the wine. All that sourness underneath –

Your dread becomes clearer. What if you get what you deserve?

But with it, the longing –
And it's so late.

6.42pm

You're calling.

The phone damp already in your hand.

But you're calling.

And between the ringing tone and your heartbeat, it occurs to you that your mobile's small glowing screen revealed no new messages. Not one missed call –

You look down at the bruises on your wrist. The bruises that I put there. And I join you in your wondering about whether I'll reply.

Rash

The rash began the night that Fran heard the news, when she was back at her father's house, which she supposed wasn't actually her father's any longer, but only hers. Because there was only her. No Father.

There had been the call from the hospital and then the rush to the station, fumbling over tickets, coins showering the concourse. And then the jogging train that had mocked her panic, its sluggish hours interrupted solely by the refreshment trolley clanking up and down the aisle.

Similar rain-soft fields rolled by outside, grey and spectral. Sometimes a horse or a pony appeared, and once, a flurry of sheep, but it was the horses who kept returning so that it was like watching the same looped footage. The drops against the window provided scratches, static, frame after frame.

Fran remembered the click and whir of cine-film and her eyelids flickered, but she didn't sleep. Nor did she cry, not then, and of course the journey wasn't truly endless, but something real because there, suddenly, was the poky, familiar station with its rust-bitten benches – benches she'd shivered on years ago, her best friend, Hazel, at her side.

Except there wasn't time for reminiscence; later, Fran supposed, some of that was bound to come, but there was the taxi to negotiate first and then the hospital itself, where uniforms fluttered about her, crisp and blue, and the ceiling lights seared white.

Once Fran had finished form-filling, she was led to a smaller room. There, the lighting wasn't quite so harsh, but the air-conditioning churned, puffing out metallic gusts. It was a shock – shocking – for Fran to see her father, but not in any way that she might have anticipated. Her astonishment was quiet. It fell through her in clumps like melting snow.

Her father's hair had been combed. It looked surprisingly silvery, scraped away from his dry forehead. Pinned beneath a starched sheet and then wrapped further in pale paper, he lay in the very centre of the bed, neat and little. Fran had never seen him look little before.

"Larger than life," that's what people said of him – not because he was gregarious, *the life and soul* (god, and god forbid), but because of his voice, which was all the more booming because mostly he was silent. And then there was his stature too – the village had always known him as a strong, brave man. Upstanding, literally, with that ram-rod spine.

Fighting disbelief, Fran wondered if there hadn't been some mix-up? Maybe that shrunken figure wasn't her father after all; she'd taken a misplaced call, completed the wrong questionnaires... It wasn't just his size, but his stillness too – although that was madness, obviously. Did she honestly expect him to go on sawing, lifting, determinedly walking, now that he was dead?

Fran found that she was holding herself soldier-rigid in response. Only her twitching fingertips betrayed her urge to reach out, to break that frozen spell by brushing her father's powdery cheek or his new glimmering hair – except that then she wondered about that impulse too. Was it driven by curiosity rather than affection? How would her father *feel* now? Like cardboard? Pastry? Candle stubs?

She remembered the waxwork museum she'd visited when holidaying with Hazel as a child, a faded seaside place crammed with giant dolls you had to squint at to recognise: the Royal Family, the Prime Minister, Mohammed Ali and John Lennon – possibly. She recalled the Chamber of Horrors, stuffed with murderers. Apart from Ruth Ellis in a lopsided wig, they were all men, weasel-like men mostly, spectacled and suited. Yet it had been disconcerting, that cluttered room; as if their creator had thought it a prerequisite, each figure had worn the same half-grin – a purple twisted smile like Mr Punch's, out on the sand.

It wasn't long before Fran had bolted, deliciously hysterical, with Hazel shrieking at her side. It was the summer when they were at their most inseparable, and unstoppably, Fran remembered other things: the single black of sea and sky beyond the pier and the thrill of eating as they strolled – steaming doughnuts, fish in batter, chips. Heading back to the hotel, to the over-blanketed bed they'd had to share, the girls had sucked hot sugar and stringent vinegar from their fingers. And everywhere, that sting of salt...

Abruptly, Fran stepped away from her father. She felt sick, sickened by his frailty, that vacancy, but mainly sick at herself. She wasn't thinking any of the right things. She couldn't touch him. In the end, she just left, nodding as she passed the desk uniforms, who scarcely glanced up from their folders.

At least, Fran told herself as she waited for another cab, her father hadn't been smiling – not like Hazel's waxworks. Like Hazel.

137

As soon as she reached her father's house – her house – Fran's exhaustion set in. She'd imagined that she might spend some time wandering the rooms, reacquainting herself with the peeling paint on the kitchen cupboards, perhaps running her hands over the dents in her father's chair. Instead she took herself straight off to her old bedroom, turning on the lights only as she needed them and clicking them off again quickly as she went. She wanted only sleep –

But in the night, the rash came.

It woke her in the way that dreams would sometimes. She was pulled into consciousness gasping, scrabbling. As if escaping some tunnel, fighting off black clods of collapsing earth. For a while, she simply lay there, breathing, feeling the rash even before she looked. It wasn't an itch or an ache, but something in-between.

When she flicked on the lamp, she saw it on her arms first. It was on both arms – white lines rising and scattering from the insides of her elbows to her wrists. Higher, towards her right shoulder, it became distinctly crosshatched. There, it reminded Fran of nettle marks, except it didn't hurt. She pushed back the eiderdown and found that her legs were equally patterned. She was laced from calves to hips.

She tugged off her nightdress and then hopped, naked, to the dressing table. She wanted to see clearly.

The ancient hinged mirror reflected back three Frans, each one streaked. Beyond her, the walls of her bedroom were a faded peach, her teenage posters removed long ago, but in the lamp's glow, the walls appeared duskier than usual and Fran also looked muted, almost satiny, despite the rash. More intrigued than concerned, she refocused.

It covered the whole of her. It littered her sides, her waist. It swirled in tribal stripes across her breasts and then fragmented on the path back to her stomach, breaking into the dot-dot-dots in a story. *Ellipses*, Fran recalled...

She wasn't a woman who usually took much notice of her body, apart from the basics, filing her nails and removing excess hair, moisturising after her longer baths. When she shared herself with boyfriends (*men-friends*, she supposed, since she'd grown older), sex was pleasant enough, or at least not unpleasant, although even when she'd begin to feel herself quicken, there was often a sense of disengagement, as if she was watching herself from afar.

Not that there had been anyone for months, no one since Christopher, who it turned out had been a messy mistake. Generally, Fran didn't like mess, disorder. She liked to keep things organised and controlled – even, she supposed, her own body. Alone, between relationships, she rarely recognised the need to touch herself.

Except now, she realised, she was sliding her hands quite unselfconsciously across her skin, searching out its new lumps and heat and cold-spots. And as she explored, Fran thought of how the rash had woken her. She relived that dream of clawing fingers, although she was no longer imagining her own, pushing up through darkness. She thought about a different kind of scurrying, emerging from inside.

In the morning, Fran felt ravenous. She swept through her father's kitchen (*her* kitchen) eating his leftovers, white-edged cheese and flaking crackers, softened biscuits by the fist-full from the tin. Chewing, she remembered sleepovers at Hazel's house, midnight raiding expeditions. She glanced down at the crumbs caught between her shirt buttons and felt the rash, still bubbling, beneath the silk.

But there was a lot to do before the funeral, and wasn't it better to keep busy? Determinedly, Fran hunched over her father's telephone and his dog-eared address book, silently rehearsing in the slow-breathing seconds between each dial.

"Hello, this is Frances Hadley. I don't know if you remember me? You were a good friend of my father, Paul. I'm afraid I have some sad news..."

Mostly, she didn't have to explain any further. Word had already slipped around the village and she frequently felt a sigh dragging at the line well before she'd finished blurting. Nevertheless, the repetition was draining.

"He was a rock," someone said. "A tower of strength," said another, and Fran felt herself grow weaker, more corroded, with each response.

After the final call, she lowered her face into her hands. Her ears were buzzing and yet the one number she'd wanted to dial, she hadn't; she couldn't. What was the point? She sat for several minutes hiding in her palms and longing to cry, except how could she? She felt fraudulent, suspecting that if the tears did arrive, they would have been misplaced.

Eventually, she rose. *Keep busy*, she remembered. And rolling her sleeves up before the sink, she saw that her arms were her own again, unblemished.

During the five days that had to pass before the funeral, Fran cleaned. She threw out the ancient food in her father's cupboards, the weevil-specked flour and clumped sugar, the faded teabags leaking burnt-looking grains. When the shelves were clear, she scoured them with an even greater vigour than she applied to her own sparse flat, already becoming unimaginable, back in the city.

Her father's military standards had obviously started to slip. There was grime in the grouting and the windowpanes were clouded. Cobwebs netted the light fittings to their shades, so when with a deep breath, Fran went upstairs to face her father's room, it was a surprise to find his bed looking as rigorously made as ever. The corners were taut and below a solitary pillow, the sheet had been turned down in a pristine panel.

She should have predicted nothing less. After all, every Sunday night, as a child, there had been the regular Room Inspections, but gazing at those decided lines, Fran understood that she'd expected something altogether different: a torn tangle of covers, the mattress exposed – signs of a struggle maybe – although frankly, that was silly. No one had actually told her that he'd died in bed.

Fran swung away, towards the wardrobe. While she couldn't bring herself to strip her father's sheets, she could, she should, do *something*. With a kind of clenched tunnel-vision, she plunged among the hangers and began dividing his strange empty clothes into two sensible piles: the still-respectable, the rags.

When the house – his house – became too much, Fran walked. She'd choose a path into the woods and keep going till she started noticing the yellowish pools in the rutted earth, the musky mushroom flavours. By the time she managed to tune in to the birdsong she was able to return – when she felt suitably removed.

But on the day before the funeral, there was more to clear from Fran's head. In her father's workshop, facing the sawdust tides, she'd dropped to her knees with a dustpan and it had returned to her, in a rush, how they'd used to pray together.

Up until Fran became a teenager, her father would bow beside her each bedtime, talking of purity and honour, sacrifice and strength. Before his rumbled *Amen*, he always left a silence in which Fran would struggle, understanding that in that space she was meant to be offering her own private pleas. She'd never known what she was supposed to make up. For a long time, she'd wanted to ask about her mother, but how could she with her father right there, next to her? Always so much more solid than any god...

Ignoring the woods that last afternoon, Fran followed the road until it forked, heading towards the farm where Hazel used to live. Hazel's family hadn't actually owned the farm – that had belonged to Mr Dawson, but they'd rented one of his leaky cottages while Hazel's parents took charge of his stables. But the farm was further than Fran remembered and as she walked, a drizzle set in. The matted fields began to look unreal; it was like being back on the train again, except that, blinking through the rain-haze, she couldn't find a single sign of horses.

She remembered them though. She remembered white striping a chestnut nose and the slow lift of hooves like treading water. But mostly, what Fran remembered was holding her fingers flat and Hazel's calm instructions while she fed them. Breath pluming on her open palm.

When Fran reached the ridge before Hazel's old cottage, she stopped.   There was no point in investigating further – considering the horses' absence, Hazel's parents were surely long gone too.   And of course Hazel herself had moved out nearly two decades ago, council-housed when she'd had the baby.

Turning back, Fran slid one hand along the dry-stone wall beside the road.   The wall wasn't actually dry, but clammy, and she thought of all the places she used to perch on, with Hazel, when they were kids.   Not just those higgledy barriers separating the fields or the station benches, but the pub wall too, where they'd loiter after school.   And although Fran struggled to recall their murmured conversations, she remembered the chill that had burnt through her skirt pleats and how Hazel had gleamed – her teeth and eyes growing luminous against the setting dusk.

When Fran woke that night, she knew that the rash had returned.   She'd dreamt it more clearly this time. Again, she rose and crossed to her bedroom mirror. Again, in the lamplight, she undressed.

The rash encased her.   More organically, she believed, than before.   *Like plants*, she realised, vines. Once more, she studied her thighs, her hips, her waist, her chest.   She uncovered branches and blossoms, furling buds.   She craned her neck and saw that her buttocks were entwined as if with ivy.   In a way, she thought, the rash was beautiful.   The thought stunned her.

In her dream, it hadn't been a garden, but language.   Hieroglyphics or Arabic, nothing that Fran could understand.   She felt scribbled on, no different from all those walls with their literal graffiti or

143

scrawling moss – and yet somehow, beneath the rash, she felt kept safe.

But when Fran woke to full daylight, she discovered that it had grown. The rash had spread to her chin and where it littered her body, it was no longer words or foliage. At best, its scrolls suggested metalwork. Barbed-wire stars blazed across her shoulders and Fran felt caged-in. Between the bars and milky blisters, her ordinary skin looked frightened. Luridly pink.

She dressed carefully, wearing long sleeves and a high collar. She left her hair down too, although it would have been more appropriate to have it pinned up for the funeral – but it wasn't enough.

Throughout the service, Fran couldn't stop thinking about the rash. She couldn't concentrate on the Reverend's words, even while she intoned the correct responses. Her jaw tingled and she imagined a lattice containing her whole face – there, for everyone to see. She bent low over her hymn book and refused eye contact. The church was full, but Fran doubted anyone would sympathise. While the pews were packed with people she recognised, there was no one there she knew.

And even at the graveside, the rash held her. Her handful of soil was nothing; her wrists felt more roughly gravelled, pebble-sharp where her cuffs pressed close.

After the service, there was the pub. The Bell, because it was her father's regular, although to Fran, it was barely recognisable. Every booth had been re-upholstered in creamy leather and in the Lounge a wide-screen displayed Sky Sports, which somehow blared, despite the volume muted.

Had her father honestly continued to visit this place every Friday? It seemed impossible – yet apparently he had, at least according to the bar staff and the old women who flustered about Fran, refilling her wine glass, despite her protests.

"To Paul!" The landlady insisted.

The woman was blowsy, a clear expanse of milky cleavage on display. A couple of younger girls worked alongside her, their bare arms golden and utterly smooth. Everyone clinked, the bar staff and the elderly ladies who, like Fran, were well covered.

It was difficult to see the old women's true faces beneath their powder, but from what Fran could glimpse of their throats, they were marked by nothing more than creases and wattles and rubbery veins.

They leant close, these women, and piled a plate for her. There was a vast quantity of food – cakes and sandwiches and lukewarm sausage rolls, which they had insisted on providing. Surveying the feast, Fran recalled similar offerings from long ago, after her mother had left. Vividly, she pictured mud-like gravy and greying carrots, the dark-baked sockets of a stargazy pie...

Although unfailingly polite, her father hadn't any patience with such hand-outs. He'd labelled the women who left them as 'terriers'. *Terrier-women*, partly because of their unruly perms, but mainly for their enthusiasm. In a rare anecdote, he'd described the dogs that he'd rabbited with as a boy – mindlessly persistent animals, forever digging. And although Fran had been just seven, she'd laughed, already learning, learning about what her father needed, and about

145

women too. Years before puberty, and way before he'd forbidden her to see Hazel, she'd been on the look-out for clues – wondering what creature might be buried in herself.

Not that these women had any idea that they were terriers. They continued toasting her father, and while Fran couldn't bring herself to eat, she could hardly refuse their raised glasses.

"To your Dad," they said. "A true gent."

Nodding, Fran kept sipping, and then gulping, although she was aware of her empty stomach and the fact that she rarely drank, and never to excess. She was always so careful – but perhaps, just for tonight, it would help. Maybe it would ease the rash, or at least her anxiety about it?

"You're a lucky girl," she was told. "They don't make 'em like that anymore."

"Salt of the Earth."

When Fran reached out to refill her own glass, the room trembled. The bottle was empty. It reeled and as she clumsily caught it, she saw that the rash had crawled up her thumb. A trail like tiny arrows, like sparrow footprints in the snow...

"Excuse me," she said, but the old women hardly heard her. She had to push through them while the ceiling lights slid into one another, stretching like glue. She couldn't escape to the Ladies; she was too scared of the mirrors there, and so she found herself stumbling on, past the television where a crowd roared in silence. She kept going, towards the wide back doors.

"Excuse me, excuse me..."

She was trapped among the smokers huddled beneath the awning. But ahead, The Bell's yard spread out into shadows as it always had. In the darkness pooled beyond the pub's glow, Fran could just make out the wall's outline, its silvery threads. Inside her dress, her skin flared.

The rash was electricity now, a burning circuit running through her. *Hot-wired*, she thought. And then she didn't know what she was thinking anymore; her head was spinning. She staggered backwards and in trying to right herself, accidentally caught one of the smokers' arms.

"Hey," said the girl.

Fran stared, and then without meaning to, began to babble.

"Hazel," she said. "The wall. That wall..."

Hazel peered at her, her eyes glossy behind red-streaked hair – only she wasn't Hazel, Fran realised, not at all. Not unless Hazel had become frozen in time, held eternally in her teens.

"Wait here," the girl replied and vanished, leaving Fran to teeter across the pub garden alone.

Weaving closer to the wall, she wondered what else she might see there. Who? Two young girls sniggering, whispering, discussing kissing techniques?

Except suddenly the wall was rushing too fast towards her. Fran was tripping, falling. Her skull rocked as her head smashed into it, but for a moment, there was no pain – and then the entire blackening sky rang with it.

Crouched on the gravel, Fran put a hand to her forehead. She couldn't feel the bumps of her rash, only an ordinary wetness. Slow-spreading blood that she could also taste, a mouthful of pennies...

"Fran?"

As the woman drew Fran to her feet, Fran saw that she was her own age. There were traces of crinkles around the woman's mouth and eyes, but her eyes – *her eyes shone*, and: "Hello!" Fran blurted.

And then they were both laughing, stupidly, recklessly – until Fran understood that she wasn't laughing at all, but crying.

Behind Hazel, in the doorway, faces bobbed. Hazel's daughter floated among them, red-streaked and wary and possibly amused.

"Come on," Hazel said. "Let's get you out of here, get you cleaned up."

In Hazel's car, Fran couldn't stop crying. The sobs prevented her from speaking clearly, although she kept wanting to, wanting to explain how these were the first tears since her father's death, but how it wasn't him that had released them, but other memories, the pier and the horses. That wall...

How, after the last time that they were there, she knew that Hazel had returned for her, that she'd kept on coming back, calling outside Fran's bedtime window, calling and calling...

Desperately, Fran wanted to explain, how she couldn't go out to Hazel, with her father sleeping in the room next door. With the sheer weight of her father's fears – fears that hadn't Hazel confirmed, with her pregnancy just a few months later?

But the tears and blood jumbled Fran's words and they became muddled with other excuses. Protestations about how she wasn't used to alcohol, how she never fell over. And she certainly never cried, *not like this –*

"Hush," Hazel said. "Hush, now. It's ok."

Slightly slurring, so that Fran wondered how much she'd also been drinking, and if that was the case, whether they were safe in the car – even now, a part of

Fran remaining cautious – although if Hazel was tipsy, might that make things better? Forgettable, if not forgivable, at least?

But then they were back at Fran's father's house – her house – with Hazel capably managing the keys and the front door, even the stairs. And while Hazel guided Fran towards her room, with one arm around her waist, Fran went on trying to apologise. She *had* to –

Except still, she couldn't speak, even with Hazel right there, with everything there – the way they'd giggled, their legs tangling in the sheets in that seaside hotel, and the pub wall of course, the shadows wrapping them like velvet when they'd pulled close.

It was startlingly clear: the cold and grit shifting beneath her – Hazel's fingertips, transforming on Fran's neck. She could picture Hazel's young face tipped back, her eyes closed – she remembered the relief of that... Until the moment when their tongues had touched and Hazel's gaze grew wide and dazzling once more –

And Fran had realised that she couldn't bear it. Not any of it. She couldn't bear that looking, that *knowing* – her father was right; Hazel was wrong. She couldn't see her anymore.

Fran had sprung away, running faster that night than ever before, chased on by a sudden wind that had sent the trees reeling, the dark hills bristling. The whole village had rippled, while something beat back, floundering, within her too, some fallen, ugly, helpless creature. A fledgling bird –

Repeatedly, Fran had tried to swallow. She'd longed for those gusts to clean her, to empty her, to drive out those other sensations. But even as she'd fled, she'd recognised her body as a trap; she'd felt those flightless wings beneath her skin –

"I'm sorry."

Finally, Fran sputtered it, and with the words, she felt herself breaking, walls collapsing. She was cracking like wax –

Except by then Hazel was preoccupied. The bleeding had stopped and now she was attempting to undress Fran, to put her to bed – and too late, Fran remembered the rash. Too late, she tried to tug back her clothes.

But Hazel's eyes were already on her, and then Hazel's hands were on her too, tracing the Braille of her skin.

"It's ok," Hazel said, her fingertips following the rash's loops and whorls – "It's all ok. I love you."

And still, it took Fran a moment to realise: she wasn't being read.

Bones

We had sex in the cave that day, or thought we had, but I knew that wasn't what caused my visitor to appear. It was because of the bones that we'd been gathering all afternoon.

Trawling the beach, we had uncovered so many. At first, they weren't much, finely lined and spined and feathery, clearly nothing more than fish. But as we continued to hunt, kicking through seaweed and shingle and then bending to rummage through dark pockets of sand, our findings grew more interesting. There were a number of bird skulls.

The ground oozed between our fingers in gritty worms as we dug them free. Gull-heads, we assumed, because there were plenty of gulls chalking the blue above – although the skulls' dimensions varied greatly. One was as small as my bitten-down thumbnail, another large and ridged as my cousin's fist. And yet they all bore the same pristine curves, the same sad sloping sockets.

Shaded cartoon-eyes, filled with nothing. Before we found the other bones, they'd seemed like a prize – truer versions of the Venetian masks that queued blindly along the shelves in our Grandfather's study. But as we continued our excavation, our treasures only grew in size and mystery.

There were three long yellowed shards, each rounded at one end, split and peeling at the other. When my cousin discovered them, he held them, in turn, against my outstretched arms, but they didn't compare. There was another, rounder and flatter, which might have been a stone, except that its honeycomb heart gave it away. And finally, we found the ribcage.

A bleached spider skulking between the oily rock-pools, it was bound with weeds like matted hair and rasped loudly against the barnacles when we wrenched it free. My teeth rattled alongside it as we dragged it down to the white horses. We wanted to wash everything clean.

"A big dog," my cousin determined.

But watching the foam hiss over his hands, his knuckles pale with grasping, I was not so sure...

But the ribcage decided us. It made a perfect centrepiece to the pattern we'd laid out before the cave's clammy mouth, and our search had to end somewhere. Besides, we were hot from our exertions. Although the sun was beginning to set, it remained fierce.

But the bones looked so beautiful, salted and shining, and arranged as they were, that it was hard to leave them. After I led my cousin into the cave I found myself glancing back at them repeatedly. The birds – the live ones – appeared fascinated too. They flickered, swooping closer, more like vultures than gulls, their shrill cries noisier than the crashing waves, the haul of shingle.

Even as my cousin, panting and squelching, climbed out of his damp trunks, I kept looking back, staring past his freckled shoulder. Finally freed, he lobbed his trunks onto the broken rocks. They landed with a smack just a foot from where my costume already lay, flesh-pink and wrinkled.

Inside the cave, we stood because the scalloped ground was too rough to lie down on. Silent and desperate, we rubbed what my mother called our 'secret parts' together. We didn't kiss, although we held each other tighter than we'd held anyone before –and there was a moment, a single moment, when he might have succeeded.

The pain made me plummet.

In that instant, my body, separate, rose and rushed to cover me, while I hid, buried somewhere deep in my own marrow. I felt both prized open and perfectly encased.

But the moment ended.

When my cousin staggered away, my thighs were sticky. I imagined that I might be covered in blood, but the stickiness was far more transparent, less definite, than that. Then my cousin, red-faced, reached for his sodden trunks, and that glistening against my skin was all that I was left with. That, and a sting like brine.

Leaving the cave, we both stumbled. Our feet caught and rolled and before we heard the snapping and crunching, we felt the splinters, the piercing intense despite our summer-toughened soles. I tasted bile.

We were trampling, destroying, all of our lovingly placed artwork – and perhaps it was the crushing rather than the bones themselves that invited my visitor.

Back at our Grandfather's house, the aunts and uncles and parents were strange and quiet. Wan and rustling, they skimmed the kitchen like paper cut-outs, careful not to scrape against one another or speak above a murmur. They had already prepared a ridiculous amount of food and yet they went on preparing more. Our hair was silted, our fingernails torn and dirty, but not one of them told us to have a bath or go to bed.

Apparently the Priest had already been called for my Grandfather. And in the end, we took ourselves off.

Lying between clean sheets only made my grubbiness more satisfying. My cousin was curled in a matching bed in the room next door, but I didn't bang on the thin wall as I'd done every evening since we'd arrived. I wondered if he might knock instead, and then because of the cave, if I knew him better now, or less so? I thought about our bare feet, our skin. The grinding of bones.

When I woke, it was into the very blackest part of the night. Beyond my rattling window, the sea wheezed, but the gulls were silent. It took several minutes for my eyes to adjust – to understand that the glimmering at the end of my bed was person-shaped.

The figure was tiny, and yet its weight pulled the covers taut across my ankles. I couldn't even wriggle my grimy, peeling toes.

I closed my eyes, and when I opened them, it was still there.

It sat, hunched, with its spindly legs drawn up to its chin and as my vision went on clearing, I saw how its head was cocked, its sallow face resting on its kneecaps.

Poised like a child and child-sized, and yet the hollows of its flesh suggested age, although it was no age that I could have guessed – as I couldn't understand its gender either. A woman, I wondered briefly, because of the sack-like dress it wore, but perhaps not. It was breast-less, and utterly hairless. Perhaps it was something in-between.

Its bald scalp, stretching from its powdery forehead, was intricately cracked, webbed, and the same off-white colour as its gown. It looked at me without blinking and its eyes, I saw, were also a tainted, tea stained white – as hard and gleaming too, as my Grandfather's crockery.

Just beyond the flimsy wall, mere inches away, I knew my cousin was sleeping. But I couldn't hear him snoring or muttering, or any of his gulped, quavering sighs; he might as well have been cast out. On a whole other island altogether.

We were enclosed, alone, my visitor and I.

Despite my tangled sheets and its heavy clothing, the figure remained clear and rigid, jaggedly pieced together. Although crooked, its jaw appeared knife-edged, its elbows spiked, and my gaze kept snagging on its ribs. Its dress, like its pallid skin, meant nothing; its true angles cut straight through. My visitor was all stalactites and stalagmites – it smelt dank too, in the same way as the caves.

And not once did it break its stare. I felt its greed.

For a long while, in that room, that night, there went on being only us. Only our need. Everything else ceased to exist; even the ocean's murmur slipped away.

But at last, I could no longer bear its staring – I clenched my whole face shut. And then, after some time had passed, seconds or years, I heard the front door slam and realised that the Priest had finally gone, but I didn't dare open my eyes again to find out whether my visitor had also left.

In the morning, there was the familiar smell of burnt toast, a scent that I'd become used to over the weeks that we had stayed – and yet everything had changed. Even the way that the dust-motes flitted on the landing had altered and long before I went downstairs, I knew.

Of course I'd gauged it already, way before the door-knock of the Priest's departure. With my night visitor, how could I not have known? And possibly even hours before that, back in the cave, I'd felt it, burrowed in my marrow.

When I sat down at the breakfast table, with my cousin sunburnt and eye-averting beside me, there was no need for anyone to mention the fact that my Grandfather had died.

"Pass the butter," I said.

And my cousin's fingers brushed mine when he handed me the dish, but I didn't flinch or wince, although I might have. For the first time understanding that all of us are bones.

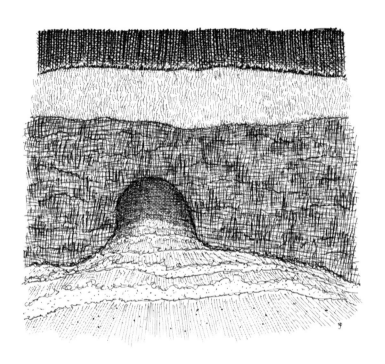

159

Acknowledgements

First, enormous gratitude to Ian Collinson for your ongoing guidance, patience, kindness and belief. It's an honour to be published by Weathervane Press.

Thank you Nikki Pinder for your enthusiasm and talent – this book wouldn't be the same without you either.

Thank you to everyone at Nottingham Writers' Studio for all your incredible support – special thanks to Pippa Hennessy and to the wonderful writers in my fiction group, Giselle Leeb, Ian Douglas, Ian Collinson (again!), Jayne Pigford and Jane Kirtley. I don't know where I'd be without your feedback and advice.

Thank you to all the brilliant writers who shared Moniack Mhor 2014, Anne Worthington, Anstey Spraggan, Louise Swingler, Anne Barber, Myriam Frey, Kerry Hadley, Danielle Jawando, Fionnuala Kearney, Emma Yates-Bradley, Stephen Galbraith, Jo Nicel and Geeta Roopnarine, and to that fine gentleman, Nicholas Royle.

Additional thanks to Steve Moran from the inspirational Willesden Herald and to the wonderful Iris Feindt, David Chadwick and Nicky Harlow from Pandril Press.

Thank you to my family and friends, the people who have been there for my writing and/or in so many other ways – thanks Giselle Leeb (again!), Lenka Galleway, Claire Pointer-Gleadhill, Bea Carrington, Pat Bryant and Caroline Smailes.

And not forgetting enormous cheers to the Taylors – to my dad, Michael, to Catherine and to Esme, and to Fred and Lola most of all.

'The Woman Under the Ground' is Megan Taylor's first collection of short stories.

Megan's third novel, 'The Lives of Ghosts', was published by Weathervane Press in 2012. Her second, 'The Dawning', was also published by Weathervane in 2010. Both novels were widely acclaimed in the press and on radio.

Megan's first novel 'How We Were Lost' was published by Flame Books in 2007 after placing second in the Yeovil Prize.

Megan lives and works in Nottingham. She is currently working on her fourth novel.

THE DAWNING

A dark and mysterious thriller set in the Peak District; the stunning second novel by Weathervane's

MEGAN TAYLOR

It is New Year's Eve, a time for fresh beginnings – but for each member of the fragmenting Haywood family, this night could mark the end.

Set against a backdrop of wintry beauty on the edge of a Peak District town, 'The Dawning' explores the danger that can arise, even at the heart of a family, over the course of one dark night.

ISBN 978 0 9562193 4 3

The Lives of Ghosts

MEGAN TAYLOR

'There were ghosts at the loch house long before we arrived with ours.'

After her parents are killed in a car accident, twelve-year-old Liberty Fuller is left in the care of her young pregnant stepmother, Marie.

Bewildered and grief stricken, Marie and Liberty travel to a remote Scottish holiday home, searching for a place to heal, but once isolated from the outside world, the girls find themselves surrendering to the dark tensions underlying their relationship.

Unable to escape their building resentment and claustrophobia and the eerie atmosphere of the house itself, Liberty and Marie are soon heading towards a tragedy of startling betrayal and further loss . . .

Twenty-five years later, Liberty's own pregnancy forces her on a journey into the past as she attempts to confront the secrets of the loch house, and the ghosts still waiting there.

ISBN 97809562193 6 7

Lightning Source UK Ltd.
Milton Keynes UK
UKOW03f0231021014

239470UK00002B/7/P